THE
Lost Saint

The Lost Saint
Text copyright © 2020 Christine Rogers
Cover and interior illustrations by Maryia Kapitsa

Published by:
Ancient Faith Publishing
A division of Ancient Faith Ministries
PO Box 748

Chesterton, IN 46304

store.ancientfaith.com

ISBN: 978-1-944967-90-1

Library of Congress Control Number: 2020944161

Christine Rogers photograph—Photographer Credit:
Camiel Hull Photography

THE
Lost Saint

Christine Rogers

ANCIENT FAITH PUBLISHING

Chesterton, Indiana

For my patient and

long-suffering parents,

Gary and Donna Young,

who have been putting

up with my nonsense and

shenanigans from day one.

Thank you for always

believing in me. —CR

CHAPTER I

June 1522

"Marko, wake up." Eleven-year-old Marko stirred and shrugged off the small hand jostling his shoulder.

"Go away," he muttered, his voice thick with sleep.

"Marko! Marko, wake up!" The urgency of her speech broke through his haze of half-consciousness. Marko forced one bloodshot eye open to see Irene, his eight-year-old sister, shaking him with both hands. She snatched them back as Marko sat straight up, his exhausted body taut with instant awareness of his sister's terror. He shook his head to clear the cobwebs from his brain and toss the black hair out of his eyes.

Irene was an early riser, usually the first of the family to awaken. Papa had built a miniature lantern for her, small enough that she could lift it easily, and she held it now at her side. The light flickered through the patterned tin and danced on the walls, illuminating her thin face and the wide brown eyes that were wild with fear. With her empty hand, she pointed silently toward the shuttered window.

Rhodes had barely begun to stir. The soft sounds of the waking city were interrupted by the bells of the nearby church of Agia Irini, startling Marko fully awake. The bells of his home church, and Irene's namesake, governed their days. They rang to mark the time, to call the faithful to services, and, as they did now, to warn of danger.

Agia Irini's bells were joined in the distance by the bells of the Catholic Church of St. Francis and the great brass bong of the largest bell in the city at Holy Trinity Cathedral. A chaotic clanging filled the air.

Marko threw off his blanket and reached blindly for his woolen breeches. They were still in a puddle on the floor where he had abandoned them in the dark early morning hours. He tied the drawstring tight with fumbling fingers and hurried to the window, flinging the rough wooden shutters open with a bang. He shivered slightly in the early morning chill.

It was one of the first days of summer, spring barely behind them, and the branches of the backyard pomegranate tree had grown long enough to block Marko's view. Reaching out impatiently, he yanked the closest branch aside, gasping slightly as a thorn stabbed the meat of his palm under his thumb. He shook the injured hand impatiently, and a few drops of blood flew through the air. Marko sucked distractedly on the wound and tried to focus.

The sun had not yet peeked over the horizon, and the predawn light was faint but brightening as sunrise crept near. From their home high on an eastern hill, he could see over the imposing stone wall that surrounded the city and all the way past it to the sea. He squinted, trying to make sense of the scene in front of him. Nothing was out of place on the white beach, but his eyes adjusted to the dimness and followed the waves as they rolled against each other, hypnotically pulling his gaze further from the shore. There, he saw them.

Ships. Not just one, but hundreds, crowded together on the horizon, a menacing smudge that extended miles in either direction and sailed closer with each wave.

Irene stood silently at his side, her dark head almost level with his own, despite the difference in their ages. His own short stature and his sister's unusual height often caused people, at first glance, to wonder if they were twins. One look at their faces usually erased the notion. Irene had weathered better the tragedy that had shaped their young lives, still wide-eyed and innocent, while Marko wore the weary, haunted look of someone aged beyond his years.

Irene stood close to her brother, nearly pressed against his side but not actually touching him. She was the only person in the whole world who seemed to understand the pain that physical contact brought him.

Marko heard the bedroom door open behind him and his mother's bare feet slap across the rough wooden floor. "Oh, Marko, you're here. Why are the bells ringing? I wish you wouldn't . . ." Her voice trailed off as she glanced through the open window over her son's shoulder and gasped. "Holy Mother of God, protect us," she breathed, crossing herself and snatching Irene into her arms in one fluid motion. "The Ottomans are invading."

An icy shiver tiptoed up Marko's spine at his mother's

words. Their island was three hundred miles off the eastern coast of Greece, and far enough away from the mainland to be easy prey for opposing armies. Year after year, marauding raiders attacked their ships at sea and threatened their population, encroaching on their fishing waters and pillaging the coastal villages. Years ago, before Marko was born, an invasion force had attempted to take over the island but had failed. Since then, enemy forays to Rhodes had been limited to three or four ships, maybe five at a time.

Marko looked again at the militant threat on the horizon. This show of force could only mean one thing. They came for war.

The front door slammed open, startling them all. "Eleni! Is Marko home?" shouted Marko's father in panic.

"He's here, Papa!" Irene called back, and his father joined them at the window.

"A messenger just came from Commander de L'Isle. It's bad," Iakovos said, pulling Irene to himself as he addressed Marko and his wife. "There are over four hundred ships. We are preparing the garrison for siege."

"What's a siege?" Irene asked, her trembling voice muffled as she hid her face in the fine weave of her father's tunic.

"The soldiers are closing the gates and locking the city down. No one will come in or go out until the assault is over. A siege," he said, setting Irene down and kneeling to look in her eyes, "is a long battle. You and your mother must work hard today to gather all of our food. Hide what you can, and bury anything of value in the garden."

"Marko, you stay here," he addressed his son sharply, noticing Marko's slight movement toward the door. "No running off today. I need you to move the chickens closer to the house and as far from the fence as you can. Clear out the sunroom and fill it with hay for the goats."

"Inside, Papa?" Marko asked, surprise interrupting his attempt to flee.

Papa nodded. "Yes, inside. The siege could last a long time, and until it ends, we are cut off from the farms outside the walls, and we won't be able to get to the ocean to fish. People will grow hungry, and I don't want the goats stolen." He paused and reached to gather his wife and daughter in a fierce embrace. "I must report to the fort. But before I go, let us pray together."

Iakovos bowed his head and tightened one arm around Irene, the other reaching for his wife's hand. Eleni made a slight motion toward her son, and Marko could read the desire in her eyes to draw him near, but he stepped back hastily, turning his gaze resolutely toward the window. She rested her hand instead on her husband's arm as Iakovos asked for God's mercy and protection in the perilous days to come. As soon as he said, "Amen," the family scattered to prepare for war.

CHAPTER 2

By the time darkness fell, Marko deeply regretted his inability to escape the house. He had labored all day in the hot sun, unseasonably warm for so early in the summer.

The chickens were comfortable in their coop. He had dragged it from the back corner of the yard by the fence and nestled the small building under the eaves of the kitchen roof. At least, he thought with annoyance, some of the chickens were comfortable. Marko had given up attempting to herd the last of the wayward birds into their sturdy abode hours ago and privately felt that if the remaining chickens were not smart enough to seek safety on their own, they deserved whatever the weather and the invaders chose to throw at them. Irene did not share his opinion of her pets and was outside cooing at the scattered flock, trying to shepherd them out from their temporary refuge in the olive trees.

Irene. His pesky, annoying younger sister had retreated into herself so deeply in recent months that she barely spoke anymore. He had never spared her much thought. She was simply there, an unchanging part of his life, relegated to the background like the buzz of a beehive he knew existed but somehow meant to avoid. It was different now, he reflected, watching her cluck back at her resettled flock as she gathered eggs in the backyard. He was her brother, her older brother, and it was his job to protect her. His shoulders slumped.

It might be his job as the eldest to protect and defend his siblings, but he had so far proven himself unable and unworthy. What would he do if Irene needed him—needed him desperately—and he floundered? The thought sank deep in his stomach, sitting like a stone. He could not bear to fail. Not again. He sighed and turned back to his work.

Their small herd of goats, surprised at their new surroundings inside the house but supremely content, rested in the former sunroom. The three nannies chewed hay placidly as their offspring, four brown babies and Marko's

favorite, a black and white, spotted troublemaker, leapt over and around them, ricocheting off the stone walls and sending into the air clouds of hay and dust. One sharp hoof came dangerously close to trampling his bare feet, and Marko jumped out of the way.

Marko had cleared the open room of all its bits of debris and unused furniture, stacking it upstairs in the nooks and crannies of the bedrooms. Sweat trickled past his loose collar and down the back of his neck, and as he lifted his arm to wipe it away, his sleeve caught. He looked down in alarm to see his cuff in the mouth of one of the goats, who was taking advantage of his inattention and chewing contentedly. Marko swatted her away with a sharp word, and she *baaahed* indignantly before wandering off in search of a more appropriate snack. He sighed and inspected the damage to his sleeve.

The loose white linen was slobbery but mostly undamaged. The goat had gnawed a small hole by the cuff, but the simple black embroidery was intact, and Marko thought it would be easily mended. He pulled a loose thread free and bent to lift the full pails of milk, groaning inwardly at the thought of many, many days of shoveling goat manure out of the room.

Marko walked slowly to the kitchen, his arms and legs aching with exhaustion as he balanced a heavy bucket in each hand. His mother bent over the stove, humming under her breath. Her long skirts swirled as she prepared the simple meal of roasted vegetables and boiled eggs. She set a bowl with a small piece of homemade feta, still wet from the salty brine, on the table for each of them. They ate the modest portions, and Irene asked for more. Eleni sighed and shook her head, reaching out a hand to smooth a small wrinkle from the pale yellow scarf Irene wore over her hair. "We must be careful, dear one," she said gently. "We do not know how long it will be until the gates are opened again and we can bring in more food from the farms outside the city. What we have must last."

Exhaustion permeated all four family members. Eleni had several long smears of dirt on her yellow apron, marring the cheerful red embroidery. She and Irene had spent the day gathering all the food and storing it in the small root cellar dug under the kitchen floor. The wooden hatch that lifted to reveal the earthen steps leading downward had been covered by a multi-colored rug and a single chair. A weak disguise, perhaps, but all they had at the moment.

Iakovos had traversed from one end of the city to the other, carrying messages for his commander and barking orders at the soldiers under his command as they scuttled to and fro, hurrying to bring provisions into the city before the gates were bolted shut. He leaned back in his chair and sighed, reaching down to rub the backs of his calves.

Marko's eyelids grew heavy, ready to drift closed of their own accord, but he forced himself into wakefulness. He needed to escape the confines of the four walls of his house, and his refuge hidden in the cliffs pulled him magnetically. He chewed his fingernail without thinking, waiting for an opportunity to sneak out, when a sound split the air. Like the breaking of a tree branch, but infinitely louder, it came once, then twice more as Irene dove under the table to hide.

He watched his mother coax Irene from her hiding place and into her lap as Iakovos said, "Cannon. They must be close enough now to fire. It has begun."

"Are we in danger?" Eleni asked. Her voice shook, and Marko could see the muscles in her shoulders tensing sharply.

"Not yet." Iakovos reached across the small table and covered her trembling hand with his own. "We're far enough inside the city wall. They are clearing the beach, making sure they can land their infantry without the worry of being ambushed in the dark."

Iakovos stood sentry by the upstairs window until dark, watching the sun set over the wall and into the water. The great stone wall surrounding Rhodes was three stories high and wide enough for soldiers to patrol in formation along the top without fear of falling over. Their home was built on one of the highest hills in the city, nearly a mile from the closest gate, granting them an unobstructed view of the beach and the Mediterranean Sea beyond.

In the dusky twilight, the ships did not appear to move, but Marko knew the waves were bringing them ever closer. When it was too dark to see out the upstairs window, Iakovos moved downstairs, lighting the lampada in front of their icons before moving a chair to sit by the front door. He sent his family to bed, telling Eleni gently, "I'm just going to stay here a bit longer," as she took Irene's hand and guided her upstairs.

The cannons fired at odd intervals throughout the night, waiting until they were almost asleep before exploding again and startling the family into complete wakefulness. Irene took refuge in their parents' bed, nestled in a tight ball against their mother, small hands clenched in fists over her ears. Marko refused comfort and paced around his small bedroom, shaking with nervous energy. During a long lull between cannon fire, he crept stealthily downstairs and peered around the corner at his father. The light from the lampada flickered, casting dancing shadows over Papa's closed eyes. Marko watched for a moment, and when his father twitched in restless slumber, he crept out the back door into the night.

Darkness was no stranger to Marko, and despite the sporadic blasts of cannons, he stealthily crept down the deserted city streets. Their priest's home was the closest landmark to his pathway out of the city: an abandoned drain, long forgotten and hidden by a fragrant but spiny-branched shrub that grew next to the city wall. The drain opening was just big enough for his slight body to squeeze through. He felt a branch dig into his leg as he entered the drain then crawled with his forearms the long way through the wall. The tunnel smelled like metal and mildew, and he heard the skittering feet of a small creature sharing the space with him. When he reached the other end, he pushed aside yet another spiny-branched shrub and tumbled into the dirt. Carefully, he listened for signs of the invaders, but all was quiet. Loping through the brush, he followed the nearly invisible path through the waving grasses to his cliffside refuge.

The cave he called his own was isolated and hidden, high above the beach and disguised by the scraggly growth of a stunted pine that clung tenaciously to the rock. The climb was treacherous, but Marko knew every foothold and safe stopping place. His only light came from the almost full moon, but in the blackness, he could also see pinpricks of light a mile away. They were the fires in the guard posts on top of the wall, where the Knights kept close watch over the city inside and out. Tonight, they had more to worry about than a single small boy escaping the city. Marko inched his way along the cliff face, and the waves crashed at the base of the rocks far below as he swung into the narrow cave entrance.

Marko sighed in relief as he collapsed on the dusty floor, finally relaxing after the brutal anxiety of the day. Here he was safe, not from enemies on ships or warriors coming for battle, but from his family—the constant reminder of his heartache and shame.

He surveyed the moonlit scene outside. The dark water rolled in and out over the sands of the narrow beach that ended abruptly at the base of the cliffs. The shoreline curved to the left and out of sight, but if Marko followed it, he would find the broad beach where he and his friends had spent most of their spare time fishing and swimming, and where Elias . . .

"Oh, Elias," he whispered into the dark, the name echoing quietly against the damp cave walls before being absorbed by the inky blackness. Marko was too tired to prod his grief any further and fell quickly asleep.

Despite his exhaustion, he woke while it was still night

and snuck from his refuge to travel the short distance home unseen. When the first pale streaks of light announced the morning, he was dirty, exhausted, and irritable, but in his own bed. The sunrise call of Irene's displaced rooster pulled him reluctantly into wakefulness, and he stumbled to the window, his brain foggy and only partially functioning. He rubbed the sandpaper feeling from his eyes and ordered them to focus as he attempted to make sense of the change of scenery in front of him.

The white sand of his beach was invisible, crowded with dingy tents flying brightly colored pennants that seemed to have materialized out of nowhere. Men by the thousands were packed into every spare space. And the ships. The ships were everywhere, anchored on the horizon as far as Marko could see. Their island was cut off from help, completely surrounded by a blockade of enemy frigates.

Marko was so stunned by the sight that he did not hear anyone approach and was startled nearly out of his skin when he turned his head and saw his father standing beside him. Papa's face wore an exhausted mask of worry and sleeplessness as he scrutinized the invasion force in front of them.

"Stay away from the city walls, Marko," his father said grimly. "Do not leave the house unless it is absolutely necessary." He reached out and grasped Marko's shoulder, shaking him sharply as Marko squirmed to escape his grip. "Do you hear me? Stay. Here."

"Papa, I'll stay." Marko rubbed his shoulder resentfully. He tried to swallow his panic at being denied his only refuge and stared out at the water. "Papa, what is going to happen? What do the Ottomans want from us?" Despite his best effort to keep it even, Marko's voice shook.

Iakovos sighed and rubbed his forehead with the heel of his hand. "What they want is our island," he said frankly. "The port in Rhodes has been fought over for years. This is the perfect stopping point for ships traveling anywhere in the Mediterranean. Whoever controls Rhodes controls the shipping routes in this part of the sea, and whoever controls the shipping routes controls the spice trade from the Orient." He glanced at Marko. "You have seen the additional Knights in the city?"

Marko nodded. The Knights of St. John had been a fixture on Rhodes for two hundred years. They were the rulers of the island, a military organization that answered directly to the pope in Rome. They were Catholic forces, living and coexisting peacefully with the Orthodox inhabitants. Churches built for both faiths populated the city and dotted the countryside. There were several hundred Knights stationed permanently at the fort, and Papa worked for their commander, Philippe de L'Isle. In recent years, more Knights had come to stand as reinforcements against the possibility of attack, a possibility that was now unfolding before them.

"I'm thankful for the foresight of those in charge," Papa said frankly. "We will need the additional men. As for what will happen, it all depends on whether the commander was able to get a ship out to call for reinforcements before the invaders cut it off. If they did, more Knights will arrive to help fight, and we might be able to drive them back. If not . . ." He did not finish his thought but sighed deeply. "There will be fighting," he said to himself. Glancing back at Marko, his forehead furrowed. He gripped Marko's arm again, his firm hand pinching nearly to the bone. "Mind me, Marko. Stay here in the house, and obey your mother."

Marko squirmed. "I always obey Mama," he muttered, twisting away.

"Not always," Papa retorted with a flash of his eyes. His gaze adjusted almost instantly, softening into a look of pronounced grief. Marko wasted no time retreating to a safe distance out of reach. He watched warily as several emotions coursed over his father's face. When Papa made eye contact with him again, his face was filled with deep regret.

"Marko," he said softly, reaching out a supplicating hand to his son.

"Don't." Marko took two quick steps backward. "I know it was my fault. You don't have to keep reminding me."

Papa sighed. "That is not what I meant."

"Of course it's what you meant," Marko replied harshly. "You've told me my whole life that *God*"—he spat the name savagely—"wants honesty and truth, that a true word is to be valued above all things. Why would you change your mind now?"

"Don't twist my words," his father said sharply. He took a deep breath and looked out the window. "Don't take your anger out on God," he said quietly. "It's not God's fault."

"Are you sure?" Marko muttered under his breath. Out loud, he replied, "Of course not. It's mine."

Papa's shoulders sagged. "Just . . . just listen to your mother while I'm gone."

"I already told you that I will," Marko said bitterly. "I learned my lesson. I'm not likely to forget it again." Spinning on his bare feet, he stalked out of the room, glancing over his shoulder to deliver a parting barb. His father stared sadly after him.

He almost turned back but was dissuaded by the sight of Papa's arm, curled into a tight fist at his side. Marko narrowed his eyes and nodded slightly, the fist confirming an unnamed suspicion lurking deep in his mind. Marko walked away without a second glance and thought maybe he heard his father sigh.

CHAPTER 3

MARKO LEARNED MORE than he had ever cared to know about warfare and fighting in the following weeks. The ships that he had first seen were joined by others, and within a month, nearly two hundred thousand men were camped on the beach, campaigning to overtake his home. The island of Rhodes only had a force of sixty-seven hundred. Seven hundred were the trained Knights of St. John, some living permanently on the island, and others had joined in recent years from places as far-flung as Spain, France, and Germany. The rest of the force was made up of natives of Rhodes—some strangers, but many men that Marko had known since infancy. They were his neighbors, fellow parishioners of Agia Irini, the fathers, uncles, and brothers of his friends. His own father was counted among them.

Nearly all were stationed in the city, trapped under

siege and unable to leave. The other small towns and farms on the rest of the island were defenseless and were the first to fall to the invading army. Marko's mother was frantic with worry for her parents, who lived outside the walls, south of the city, a day's walk away.

Skirmishes were a daily occurrence. The Gate of St. John, the primary entrance into the walled city and named for the Knights who defended it, was the main battleground. While men fought and died, the Ottoman Sultan, Suleiman the Magnificent, sent squadrons around the wall to attack other gates at random, all the while firing cannon shot continually from ships anchored in the shallows. Most had no effect on the ramparts; the stone was tall, thick, and sturdy. The cannon shots that made their way over the walls into the city were a different story. The civilian death toll mounted, and nonmilitant citizens were forced to form their own fire brigades and struggled to dig their neighbors from the rubble of collapsed buildings.

Papa was high in the chain of command, one of the chief aides to Commander de L'Isle and directly involved in the planning of the city's defenses. He spent many late nights working at the fort and others at the kitchen table, poring over maps and schematics. Marko sat opposite him one evening, carving a small piece of driftwood that he had brought home long before the siege began.

Mama set a steaming cup in front of Papa. It wasn't coffee. They had run out of that weeks ago. But Irene faithfully tended the herbs in the garden and had picked some fresh mint that day, which Mama steeped in hot water and scantily sweetened with a hint of the hoarded honey stored in their pantry.

Papa took a brief sip and sighed. "They're digging," he said to Mama, pointing at the map. "Here, here, and here. We don't know why."

"Is there a way to find out?" she asked him.

He blew on the hot liquid. "The only way I can think is to send men in as spies, but they watch the gates as closely as we do, and if we attempt to open them even slightly, our men would surely be immediately killed."

"Can't we go over the wall?" Marko asked.

Papa looked up in surprise. "How?" he asked.

"Use ladders."

Papa smiled. "That's an idea, but I don't see how we could lower ladders long enough without them noticing, even if we did it at night. Even in the lowest points, the wall is over thirty feet high. And if they did see them, the enemy could potentially climb them before we would have a chance to haul the ladders back up."

"But you wouldn't have to use regular ladders," Marko argued. "We use ropes in the trees all the time. You could let down a rope ladder without being noticed and pull it up right away until you needed to bring your soldier back over the wall. If the enemy did see it, you could just cut the rope before they had a chance to climb."

Papa stared at him blankly then blinked owlishly and let loose a single short laugh. "Why didn't we think of that?" he asked himself, studying the maps again. He muttered questions and answers under his breath, so deep in thought and caught up in planning that he abandoned his tea. Mama passed it to Marko, who drank deeply, savoring the faint sweetness. He passed the unfinished cup back to his mother, who placed it back in Papa's hand as he groped blindly for it. He finished the now-cooled liquid and said under his breath, "This could work." Glancing up, he looked squarely at Marko and said, "Thank you, son."

Marko felt the birth of a long-forgotten glow in his belly at the words. When was the last time Papa had called him "son"? He leaned forward, eager to be of further service.

Papa was pointing out other places to Mama. "We've blockaded here and here. This spot was an old drain that we filled with rocks and where we now have a guard posted, in case they try to enter through there."

"What about the drain by Father Anthony's house?" Marko said without thinking.

Papa glanced up. "What drain?" he asked sharply.

Too late, Marko realized his mistake. His previous delight vanished, leaving a noticeable emptiness behind. "What drain?" Papa demanded.

There was no way out. "There's a drain in the wall by Father Anthony's house," Marko said in a monotone voice, bidding a final, regretful farewell to his cave.

Papa blew an exasperated breath of air through his

lips. "And you're just now deciding that it's a good idea to tell me?"

Marko had no response. He beat a hasty retreat to the backyard, leaving Mama to pacify his grumbling father.

In the days that followed, he heard snatches of conversation between his parents. The rope ladders had worked. The spies sent over the walls had found tunnels that the Ottomans were digging under cover of night, and Commander de L'Isle stationed soldiers on the insides of the wall in case they succeeded. Papa also loudly told Eleni of an afternoon spent overseeing the workers who filled in the drain near Father Anthony's house, and Marko grieved the loss of his refuge.

Their lives were filled with combat, but mealtime was a battle of a different kind. Supplies dwindled, and their animals grew thin. There was only so much grass in their small yard for the goats to eat, and the chickens who subsisted on grubs and scraps from the family's table found themselves without scraps. Every day, the goats gave less milk. Two of the nannies stopped producing altogether, and the family was forced to eat them. Four of the kids had been traded to neighbors for olive oil and other staples that had run low, and Marko was oddly grieved each time one was led away bleating. The only baby remaining was Shadow, his favorite spotted troublemaker.

Eleni and Irene tended their backyard garden fastidiously, keeping the family in vegetables, but the main harvest would not come for some time. Marko tried to stay out of the garden entirely, as the temptation to eat the tiny plants grew stronger as his belly shrank. Eleni strictly rationed the remnants of last year's potatoes and turnips, but without the influx of food from the larger farms outside the city, they lived every day wanting more.

Mama took refuge in church, attending every service no matter the hour. Most days, Irene went with her, and every time, Mama asked Marko if he would go as well. The first time she asked, Marko laughed without thinking, but he regretted it as soon as he saw her face fall. He declined politely after that. Marko knew she prayed daily for him to consent to join her, but Marko was far too angry with God to even consider setting foot in Agia Irini. Instead, he waved goodbye to his mother and sister and savored each stolen moment of silence until they returned.

Irene had abandoned their bedroom weeks ago for a permanent pallet on their parents' bedroom floor, but Marko refused to join her. Robbed of his nocturnal wanderings, he took refuge in the sunroom with the remaining goats, where he woke from nightmares of crashing ocean waves and the sound of screaming. He would sit against the stone wall, dust and bits of hay tickling his nose, Shadow clutched in his arms until his silent sobs receded and his body stopped shaking. Most mornings, he would wake on the stone floor where had he drifted in and out of sleep during the night.

This night, sleep eluded him, and dust clung to the inside of his mouth, drying his tongue and crunching like grit between his teeth. He crept to the kitchen for water, but instead of finding it empty, he overheard his parents conversing in low tones.

". . . to Ierissos?" Papa said. "Do you think they made it out?"

"Oh, Iakovos," his mother groaned. "I hope they left. And they would have gone to Diana. It's the only safe place, really."

"If we are evacuated, it's where we will go too. If de L'Isle puts me on a ship, I will have to obey orders. I won't leave without you and the children. But if we're separated somehow, go to your sister's."

Eleni sighed sadly. "The children. If only we could take them all."

"Oh, my darling. We will take Marko and Irene." He paused and swallowed hard. "And Elias . . . We will leave Elias in God's hands."

"In God's hands," Eleni echoed wistfully, looking out the dark window. "I want him here, in *my* hands." She laid her arms on the table, palms open in supplication. They shook slightly as tears welled in her eyes, spilling over the boundary of her lashes and trickling down to drip off her chin. "I want my baby, Iakovos." Iakovos reached over and gripped her hand tightly—so tightly that Marko could see his knuckles whiten with the effort, but Eleni did not move.

"I ask myself, every day," she whispered, "every day, a hundred times a day. Why did I send him with Marko? Why didn't I keep him with me, safe?"

Iakovos made a strangled sound and laid his head on the table. Eleni ignored him, staring at her empty hands. "I wanted to rest," she said softly. "He begged, pleaded to go with Marko and his friends. I knew Marko was annoyed, but I didn't think . . ." She trailed off. "It wasn't his fault," she finally finished, but her voice was unsure, as if she didn't know whether her words were a question or a statement.

"Wasn't it?" Iakovos mumbled, his face buried in his arms.

Marko heard him clearly, and the words pierced through him, so sharp and so deep that he looked down automatically, expecting to see his heart bleeding out of a wound in his chest.

His mother glanced in his direction, drawn by the movement. Marko saw panic in her eyes as she spotted him in the shadows. She reached out a hand, but Marko was quick and ducked out the door before she could call his name. He stood in the dark yard, staring at the rising moon and heaving deep breaths of sea air to calm the tumult in his stomach.

"Marko?"

Marko waited a long time to answer, not trusting his voice. Finally, sure that it would not crack, he replied. "Yes, Mama?"

"I brought you some water." Her tentative voice stabbed his swollen and crippled heart. He wanted to tell her, to shout out that he was sorry, so sorry. That he would give his whole life to go back and relive that horrible day, that he would trade places with Elias in a heartbeat. But fear glued his lips together, stopped the words from coming, because . . . what if she agreed? What if she thought, too, that it would be better if Elias were here instead of him? That if she had been forced to choose which of her sons to have in her arms, it would not have been him?

So he said nothing, except for a quiet "Thank you." He accepted the glass and drank deeply, as much to quench his thirst as to avoid talking. He felt his mother's featherlight touch on his unruly hair and flinched. His mother sighed. "Will you come inside?"

He nodded and followed her soft footsteps into the house but did not go to his own bed. Instead, he nestled into the dwindling stack of hay in the goat byre and woke the next morning covered with his mother's cloak.

CHAPTER 4

MARKO LINGERED OVER BREAKFAST the next morning, trying to make every morsel last. Irene inhaled her own small portion and rose to heat water for washing. Marko's gaze followed her as she worked. Though nearly identical in height, Marko and Irene looked almost nothing like each other. Irene possessed the small snub nose and delicate features of their father, her hair a chestnut brown that lightened with red streaks during the summer when she forgot her scarf while playing in the sun. Her cheekbones had grown more pronounced as she thinned, and he was momentarily caught off guard. Glancing from her face to his parents' faces, Marko saw that all of his family's naturally thin faces had grown gaunt under the forced rationing of the siege.

Papa rose laboriously from the table and handed his dish to Irene. He moved more slowly each day, his joints swelling and his muscles wasting. Irene smiled up at her father, and Papa rested a hand gently on her head in passing as he kissed Eleni and thanked her for the meal. Mama smiled faintly at the familiar compliment while Marko studied her face.

There were no mirrors in their home, but Marko didn't need one. His whole life he had been told how he was the miniature version of his mother, sharing everything from the broad planes of her forehead to the shining hazel eyes and coal black hair. The only clear difference was the ragged scar Marko had over his left eye, a remnant of a tumble out of a tree two summers ago. A wayward branch had scratched a deep wound, and it gushed hot blood that ran down his face and obscured his vision. Marko had been lucky—the scar was a hairsbreadth from his eye.

Eleni reached for the brightly painted pottery bowl that held the week's batch of bread rising inside of it. She had mixed the dough early in the morning, leaving it to rise on a shelf near the stove. The shelf was special to Marko; two years before, he had overheard his mother telling a neighbor that it was hard to find a place on the table that stayed consistently the right temperature for the dough to rise. He had cut the wood himself, enlisting Irene's help to show him where the best spot in the kitchen was to be found, and Papa had helped him hang it while Mama was at the market. Later that year, Marko had presented his mother with the bowl he had been given by a neighbor in exchange for several days of hard work. Mama had smiled and cried, and she mixed bread in it each week without fail.

Mama turned the dough out of the bowl and began to knead it on the wooden table across from Marko. Her black hair was pulled back from her face, tucked under a dark blue scarf that tied behind her head. Her cheeks were long and narrow, lacking the plumpness that Papa and Irene possessed, and her chin tapered to a soft point. Marko ran a hand over his face, feeling those same shapes echoed in his own bones.

Eleni hadn't slowed in her work since the siege began. She governed the kitchen and gardens with a brisk efficiency that Iakovos had commented the toughest general would envy, but the fire in his mother's eyes had dimmed.

She no longer sang while she worked, and Marko realized that those small snatches of sound had acted like a compass. He had always known where to find her, had always been able to follow her voice to where she was. Now he stumbled across her at odd moments, tripping and running into her with no warning. It was unnerving. She was quiet now, turning the bread and pressing it with the palms of her hands. There was rhythm to her work, but Marko missed the music.

The strain of life under siege had caused Mama's clear olive skin to break out in angry red patches that stretched from her hands to her neck. When they first erupted, she brushed aside her family's concern and sent Irene to pick large handfuls of chamomile from their backyard garden. Mama washed them carefully and plucked the heads of the flowers, simmering them gently in a pan of olive oil. When the oil had cooled, she strained the mixture through a cloth, squeezing out the last drops and releasing a flowery, herbal scent that filled the kitchen. She mixed the oil with beeswax gathered from his grandparents' hives last fall, and rubbed the salve into the scaly skin of her arms.

She used it several times a day, leaving behind a soft smell wherever she walked, and her skin slowly began to heal.

Mama finished forming the dough into loaves and set it back on the rising shelf. She reached for her salve on the windowsill and scooped a small portion onto her hands, releasing more of the ever-present scent of chamomile and honey into the air. When she had finished anointing herself, she reached to tuck a stray hair behind her ear. With a start, Marko noticed a streak of bright white under the edges of her scarf. It had not been there yesterday.

Every day, Suleiman's forces bombarded the city walls with cannon shot, using it as cover fire as they sent infantry to try and force their way into the city. The family grew accustomed to going about their daily tasks to the sound of artillery. Marko kept to his chores and to himself during the day, but at night he snuggled with the two remaining goats, the sound of cannons echoing across the waves of his nightmares.

Iakovos kept them apprised of events, reporting each evening what had happened that day, but Marko was sure that he edited the news, not wanting to frighten Irene.

His suspicions were confirmed when a lieutenant came to report to his father one evening after dinner. Mama, Papa, and Irene were still at the table in the kitchen. Mama shooed Irene out, but neither parent noticed Marko in the back of the room. He held perfectly still, not wanting to betray his presence, and listened to the grim account.

The fighting was brutal. Men fell constantly, giving up their lives in dozens and scores as they resisted the onslaught of enemy forces determined to break their way into the city. Today, forty men had died. The lieutenant handed his father a copy of the casualty list, mentioned something about a "body brigade," then saluted wearily before seeing himself out. Iakovos read the list, sinking into a chair. He leaned back when he was done, resting his head against the wall behind him, and the list fluttered out of his limp hand.

Eleni rested a hand on her husband's shoulder, and Iakovos looked up. "I know all of these men," he mumbled.

She made several soothing noises, and they began to murmur. Marko heard snatches of prayer from the memorial service. "With the spirits of the righteous made perfect, give rest to the souls of your servants, O Savior . . ." Eleni picked up the list and read the names in a trembling voice. Her voice hitched when she reached their neighbor Anastasio, and again when she read the name of Marko's friend Makarios's father. Marko's stomach twisted into a knot.

When they had finished, Eleni held her husband close. His voice was muffled in her shoulder. "So many men have died at that gate, Eleni. The stones are stained, dark with blood. They may never come clean." She made a choking noise, and lifting her eyes, she spied Marko. Emotion played across her face, beginning with dismay and ending in resignation. "Makarios's father died today," she said quietly.

He nodded. "I heard."

He walked toward his parents. Iakovos looked numb, and Marko wondered how many times they had done this: read a list of the dead, of their neighbors and friends, and prayed for their souls before getting up and carrying on.

"What is a body brigade?" he asked quietly.

Iakovos sighed. "Volunteers," he said flatly. "They go out at night to collect the bodies." He stood. "I have to report tonight," he told Eleni quietly, and left without another word.

"Why does he have to go?" Marko asked his mother as she watched Papa's retreating back. She looked at Marko sadly. "It is his turn tonight," she said quietly. "Papa is not really a soldier. He is a secretary, and being such, I thank God he does not fight. But this is how he honors those who do and those who die each day. He must help. You know that."

Marko fought back the bile rising in this throat. "Why did that soldier come to Papa? That hasn't happened before."

Mama sighed. "Because the chain of command is broken," she said frankly. "So many officers have died that they don't know who to report to anymore." She looked sadly at the door. "I need to check on Irene."

She left the room, and Marko picked the abandoned list off the floor. He read it from top to bottom, swallowing heavily at each familiar name. He recognized seventeen of them. Some of them he knew well, like Makarios's papa, others less well, like the Spanish Knight who frequently guarded the southern gate. They used to see him when they left the city to visit his grandparents. Marko had liked that soldier. He always winked when they passed and called out greetings in his strangely accented Greek. Irene would giggle, and the Knight would salute her and tell her she was pretty, while making his accent even more outrageous. Mama often gave him something to eat from their basket.

When Marko reached the end of the list, he closed his eyes tightly and breathed in hard through his nose, holding the breath as long as he could. When he could stand it no longer, he exhaled in a loud huff. He glanced once more at the list in his hand, and without a second thought, threw it into the fire.

The fire caught the edges of the paper in an instant. The flames ate it hungrily, and the paper blackened and crumpled into ash.

ONE AFTERNOON, four months after he had first spied the ships on the water, Marko was in the root cellar with his mother. They were gathering the remains of their food:

a few withered squashes and the last of the olives. Marko grimly gave the latest head count for the animals. "Only five chickens left," he told his mother. "We've eaten most of them, and the neighbor's dog got into the coop that time and got the others."

"Keep them alive, no matter what," Mama sighed. "We need the eggs." She opened her mouth to say more, but her words were drowned by a new kind of explosion—bigger, and far closer to home. Marko's head snapped up in alarm. He climbed the earthen steps back into the kitchen. Racing up the stairs two at a time to his parents' upstairs bedroom, he looked out the west-facing window at the cloud of dust and dirt that had appeared on the city's skyline. Sounds of panic reached him from the street.

"They have blown a hole in the city wall," his father told his mother bleakly when he arrived home after sunset. "They dug a tunnel under the fortifications and lit fuses with gunpowder from the cannons. Our remaining battalion has rallied and is defending the breach, but we don't have enough men, and no ships can make it through the blockade with reinforcements in time to help."

"What will happen?" Eleni's voice was low and trembling.

"We will have to surrender. Soon. Our forces are too depleted. I watched the troops assemble last night, and there are less than two thousand left. Two thousand, Eleni! Even the Knights are depleted. Commander de L'Isle says his count is at less than two hundred. I've overseen the burial of so many. My friends . . ." he trailed off. "How can only two thousand men defeat such a force?" His voice was flat, empty of all emotion save exhaustion and incomprehension. Iakovos ran his hands over his head, leaving his hair in disarray and unveiling the raw desperation on his face.

"There is no more food," he said in a low voice. "The army has eaten everything. If we do not surrender, we will starve—all of us and the Ottomans together. Our only prayer is that their leaders are lenient in their demands."

"Then let us pray," Eleni said, gathering Irene in her arms. Iakovos wrapped his arms around them and looked long at Marko, holding out a tentative arm in invitation. Marko held his ground, solidly out of reach, looking out the window. He had nothing to say to God. Iakovos sighed, bent to kiss Irene on the head, and Marko's family bowed their heads without him.

CHAPTER 5

"Marko!" Marko heard his name from the front of the house. "Coming," he called back, dusting off his hands and following his mother's voice.

Eleni was saying goodbye to a man Marko had never seen before, who was leaving in a rush. She bit her bottom lip and looked at Marko with a worried face. "That man has a home near the southern part of the city," she told him. "All the soldiers have been pulled from patrol to fight. Your father had asked him to report if he saw anything suspicious on the other side of the wall." She held up a folded piece of paper. "He has written this out for Papa and says he needs to be told right away. He had to hurry back home and couldn't take it all the way to the fort." Eleni squeezed her eyes shut and ran a shaky hand over her face. When she opened her eyes again, Marko could read her decision. "You must take this to him."

Marko stared at his mother. He had not been permitted out of their yard for weeks. Eleni handed him the paper and turned to wrap a small piece of bread in fabric and twine. "Take this as well. They will not feed him at the fort, and he must eat something."

Marko tucked the meager piece of bread and the folded paper into the pocket cleverly hidden inside his shirt. He slipped his feet into the simple leather shoes he wore outside the house and turned to the door.

"Take a knife," Eleni ordered. "And come home straightaway."

Marko swallowed his simultaneous fear and hope of escape from the prison that his home had become. He picked a medium-sized kitchen knife and tucked it into the specially sewn loop on his belt. "The city is desperate," Mama said quietly. Marko nodded.

The day before, he had seen two of his neighbors wrestling in the street, fighting over a withered fig. The fight had ended only when one man had bashed the other's head on a cobblestone. The winner claimed the battered fruit. The loser eventually stumbled home bleeding.

Marko headed down the quiet road. After seeing the violent altercation between their neighbors, most people had chosen to stay in their homes, figuring it was better to starve than to die in the street.

The salty sea breeze was tinged with dust and the acidic tang of gunpowder. Marko sneezed as he made his way to the fort, wishing that he was headed for his cave instead. Monochrome stone buildings blended in with cobblestone streets, and Marko wondered, not for the first time, why every stone that made up Rhodes was the same dusty taupe. On visits to his grandparents, he had seen stone buildings built with an array of earthen colors, ranging from white to dark, with varying shades of green and brown mixed in. Here, the only break in the monotony was the bright blue sky winking between the stone arches that covered alleyways and connected buildings chiseled from the same uniform blocks. Weaving in and out of the piles of rubble left from months of continuous cannon shot, he was almost to the commander's office where Iakovos worked when a great shout arose in the courtyard of the fort.

There was a sudden rush and stampede of people, and Marko was caught in the panicked melee. Frightened, he tried to fight his way out of the crush of bodies, but they packed around him so tightly that Marko could not get free. He was picked up by the force of the mob and carried away from the fort.

Marko tried to make sense of the conversations around him, but hundreds were shouting at once, and he could only pick out bits and pieces as people tried frantically to be heard.

"The army is in the city—"

"—defeated the last of our soldiers—"

"—demanded surrender or he'll kill everyone—"

Marko elbowed the crushing crowd around him. "Excuse me," he mumbled. No one listened.

Terror gave him strength, and Marko gave up on politeness. "Get out of my way," he bellowed, kicking and fighting. He searched for a break in the mass of people, stamping on toes and ignoring the angry shouts around him. He fought his way to the edge of the street and pressed into a doorway to survey the chaos.

Every civilian in sight was fleeing. In the distance, Marko could see the brightly colored flags from the beach advancing up the street. The enemy army was inside Rhodes, marching grimly on the fort. He looked around in increasing panic for a way to escape. Glancing up, he saw a porch railing directly above the door. Marko quickly climbed a nearby bench. He stretched, reaching for the porch, but his fingers just brushed the wood. He abandoned caution and leaped wildly, knocking the bench into the crowded street as he clung to the rails. His sweaty hands curled around the weather-beaten wood, and he hoisted his slight frame over the railing and into the house. The effort sapped all of his strength, and Marko lay panting on the floor.

No one was home. Marko fled through the back door into a narrow alley. The further from the fort he ran, the fewer people he encountered. But he was unfamiliar with this part of town. He looked wildly up and down, trying to get his bearings and calm himself enough to formulate a plan.

Enemies in the city. He had to get out. Away.

Marko hiccupped a sharp breath and staggered after the other people in the street. Papa told him—

At the thought of his father, Marko stopped abruptly, nearly falling over in his haste. Papa was at the fort, the same fort where thousands of enemy soldiers were now marching to demand surrender or death. He felt the message folded and hidden in his pocket. Mama said it was important, but how important? Enough to risk the chaos erupting around him? He had no clue, but his desire to be at his father's side outweighed all else.

He turned to retrace his steps, but he was lost. He spun in a circle. His thoughts raced and piled over each other at such a frantic pace that he couldn't keep up with them. His panic rose, and he turned again, thinking instead to run home, but none of the streets were familiar. There were no recognizable landmarks. He wasn't high enough above the wall to see the ocean and get his bearings. Marko shook his head violently, fiercely trying to beat back the fear hammering away at his senses.

Marko huddled in an unfamiliar alley that ran along the edge of the wall, listening to the screams and shouts that were growing steadily closer. Hot tears squeezed out of his eyes, and Marko dashed them away angrily. He was weary of fear. There had to be a place of safety, not just from the soldiers and imminent danger—but from his past and all that haunted him. He wanted someplace where he could stop being afraid, even just for a moment.

It wasn't his home; he knew that. He had been trapped there for months. Home was full of memories, of pain, and the lurking horror of his own failure. Marko felt like a piece of stone—that if one more hint of heartache chiseled away at him, he would break along the fault lines and crumble into dust. An image stirred, floating to the forefront of his mind. His cave on the cliff, high above the waves, remote. Quiet. Solitude. Safety.

Marko eyed the boundary wall. In this area, it rose three stories high and was nearly eight feet wide. Built from the same uniform stone as the rest of the city, it loomed before him, the only obstacle between himself and the edge of the sea, an impenetrable barrier, interrupted only by guard towers built at even intervals along the top.

There was no way over the wall. Even six months ago,

before rationing and fatigue had withered away his muscles, Marko never could have made it. It was the consum-
mate joke among his friends, before the accident, at least.
Before the presence of his friends reminded him of the
worst day of his life. They would dare each other to climb
the wall, then hoot with laughter and punch each other
in the arm. Now and then, one brave soul would make
an actual attempt, and once Marko had seen his friend
Makarios make it nearly fifteen feet high before losing his
grip and falling into the bushes. He had emerged scraped
and bleeding—but victorious. No one else had ever
climbed that high since. Marko wondered if Makarios still
tried climbing, but then he recalled Makarios's father's
name on the list of the dead.

Marko banished the thought of his cave from his mind.
Like it or not, he would have to head home. He squinted
at the sun and picked the direction he thought was toward
his house. He followed the inside of the wall, weaving
between the cypress and bay trees that grew wildly along
the stone barrier. If he followed the wall long enough, he
would eventually stumble across one of the eleven city

gates. They were heavily guarded in the best of times, and at the worst were piled high with bodies like the blood-stained Gate of St. John. Marko shivered. Bodies or no, gates meant guards, and guards could point him home.

The popping explosion of nearby guns interrupted his thoughts, and Marko flinched, reminded of the cannon fire that kept him awake at night and infiltrated his dreams. That memory triggered another—and Marko had not realized its ramifications until this moment. The army had entered the city because they had blown through the stone barrier with explosives.

There was a hole in the wall.

CHAPTER 6

MARKO STOPPED WALKING as the thought struck him, and he stood, mindlessly chewing on his fingernail, mulling through the possibilities. The hole in the wall would be heavily guarded and perhaps the scene of battle. The odds of a child sneaking past a battling army without injury were impossibly small, and Marko had enough value for his life not to want to attempt it.

He turned in the other direction but leapt back as two bodies crashed into the building in front of him. He scrambled behind a sturdy cypress tree that stood some distance from the wall and chanced a terrified look at the scene in front of him.

Two men were fighting to the death. The first was a Knight of St. John. His black tunic emblazoned with a white cross was ripped and filthy. The Knight ducked from a vicious swipe from his enemy. He breathed heavily, his sword held ready, and his eyes locked on his opponent.

The man he fought was tanned and scarred, with a turban wrapped around his head and a crossbow slung across his back. He wielded a curved blade longer than Marko's arm, and he expertly spun the sword in a fierce arc. He had the advantage, and he knew it. He spat out a string of taunting words in an unrecognizable language, and the Knight sagged, knowing defeat was near.

The Knight looked up. He appeared only a little older than Marko, his face streaked with dirt and splattered with blood. With growing horror, Marko realized that he knew this particular Knight. His name was Enzo. He was a twenty-six-year-old Italian—who possessed a bitter sense of humor that was a direct result of years of teasing from the other Knights because he looked ten years younger than he was. Enzo worked under Papa and had been invited to Marko's home on several occasions. Marko couldn't stand him. He was self-righteous and smug, frequently teasing Irene about spots on her nose and challenging Marko to mock duels at which Enzo cheated when Papa wasn't looking.

Marko didn't like Enzo, but that didn't mean he wanted Enzo to die. He glanced back at the invader, who had stuck his curved sword in the ground and leaned forward, resting on the hilt. Marko could suddenly look past the fearsome grin and wild eyes and see the invader as another boy, not that much older than himself, fear showing in cracks through the swaggering bravado. He never knew that armies were made up of soldiers so young. Would either of them live to see the end of the day?

Enzo spotted Marko crouched behind the tree, and his battle-weary eyes widened. He glanced back at his foe and without a moment's hesitation turned and ran, leading his challenger away from Marko and back to the heart of the battle. The Ottoman soldier hefted his sword out of the dirt and wearily chased after Enzo without a backward glance.

Marko's shaking legs collapsed beneath him, and he fell to the ground. He had been right about the battle being focused on the hole in the wall and had unwittingly stumbled across that very spot. He could see the damage from his hiding place, a jagged semicircle of stone missing, like a toothless gap in a smile. Huge blocks of monochromatic Rhodesian stone littered the ground, and the wall above his head was blown apart in pieces.

Enzo had fled, chased by his opponent, but dozens still fought around Marko, swerving between trees and in the open swath of land by the wall. Swords clashed and men shouted in foreign and familiar languages, but when they died their screams all sounded the same. Marko was rooted to the spot, petrified. Enzo had saved his life, but it wouldn't stay saved for much longer if he didn't find a place to hide.

There was nowhere to go but up. He reached to the branches above him, ascending with the practiced ease of one who had spent many hours at home high in the trees. The top of the tree was thin, wobbly, and patently unsafe. If he had been playing with friends, Marko would never dare to scale this high, but the uncertain danger of the tree was infinitely better than the certain danger of the battle raging on the ground below. Marko climbed.

He was level with the top of the wall when he stopped to catch his breath. The tree shook alarmingly. The fighting was closer, and two men fought each other just below him, slamming into the base. Marko grabbed the trunk and held on.

The clamor of battle—shouting and screaming, clashes of metal on metal—filled his ears, and Marko's whole existence shrunk to nothing more than the branch he clung to and the blood he could smell in the air. He was almost senseless with terror. If men continued ramming the tree, there was a good chance he would be jarred from the branches and fall. If the fall didn't kill him, landing in the middle of full-blown combat certainly would. He frantically searched for somewhere, anywhere he could go that was away from here.

His gaze landed on a branch that stretched a spindly bough over the top of the wall. It would never support an adult, but Marko was slight to begin with, and months of siege rations had left him even skinnier. There was a good chance it would hold him. Marko reached a shaking arm and climbed the last few feet to his goal. Lying on his belly, with his feet pointing at the stone barrier and his face against the scratchy bark of the cypress trunk, he wrapped his arms and legs around the branch beneath him. Slowly pushing backward, he wiggled down the thinning bough, which drooped alarmingly. Marko had the equally alarming thought that perhaps this was a bad idea, but the battle below him roared on. There was no going back.

Marko held on to the narrow hope that the fighting would prevent anyone from seeing his precarious attempt at escape. He was close now, the sagging branch working marginally in his favor to lower him closer to the wall. He scooted another inch, then heard the unnerving crack of splintering wood. Without a second thought, he shimmied backwards as fast as he could, not feeling the scrapes and splinters inflicted on his torso and hands. Marko flung himself off the teetering branch as it fell from under him. Landing with a thud on top of the wall, he tumbled along the narrow battlement until he was abruptly stopped by the guard hut that jutted up from the stone fortification.

He lay flat on his back, arms flung out limply beside him and his head turned to the side. He was astonished to be alive. The branch he had clung to was broken and hanging by several threads of splintered white wood. As he contemplated the utter lunacy of the last ninety seconds, he heard a final, definite snap. The last sliver broke and the branch crashed down the side of the cypress, landing with a thump. Marko heard an anguished howl below, and he had room in his spinning mind only for a disjointed hope that whoever had been crushed by the falling wood had not been on his side.

Marko crawled to the edge and peeked down. The battle still boiled below. The ground was littered with unmoving soldiers, and a few unfortunate souls who weren't dead yet but lay moaning in pools of blood. Marko ducked back. He was too exposed up here on the wide-open wall.

Marko climbed to his feet and pressed his body flat against the hut. It reminded him of the squat stone shed Papa had built in their backyard. Barely a single story high with wide, arched holes on each side, it gave the guards an unimpeded view in every direction. He peered cautiously through the stone window closest to him.

The single guard inside was absorbed in the battle below but ripped his sword from its sheath without hesitation when he spotted Marko. He stopped in mid swing when Marko cried out in Greek.

"What?" the soldier sputtered. "A child? Where did you come from?"

He grabbed Marko by the back of his shirt and hauled him inside the guard post. "What are you doing here?" he demanded, dropping Marko in a sprawl on the floor. Marko pressed himself into the corner and held up his hands in self-defense.

"I got caught in the fighting," he babbled, tripping over his words in petrified haste. "I climbed a tree, but it was shaking, and broke, and I jumped and landed on the wall and can't get back down"—he hiccupped and pointed a shaking finger toward the blood-soaked ground—"because everyone is dying."

The guard heaved a loud breath. "Well, you can't stay here!"

Anger boiled through Marko's midsection. "Then where do you think I should go?" he demanded.

The guard opened his mouth but his words were drowned out by the continued clashing of swords and screaming of men. He snapped his jaw shut and jerked a head toward the back wall of the hut. "Sit," he growled.

Marko slumped to the floor, wrapping his arms around his legs and leaning against his knees. What now?

Papa had taken him to a guard post like this once, showing him the spectacular and unimpeded view. The guard he had met that day was jovial, laughing with Papa and allowing Marko to drop a ripe melon over the side just for the simple pleasure of watching it splatter on the ground.

Marko glanced at his companion. The man's mouth was set in a thin line, and the deep furrow between his eyes lent him an overall look of grimness. Marko couldn't blame him. His friends were battling on the ground without him. Their forces may have been depleted, but the soldiers fought for their homes and their families and would not easily give up.

A stone bottle of water sat nearby. Marko reached for it and paused when the soldier looked sharply at him then grunted permission. Marko tipped the bottle to his mouth. It was warm, but it was wet, and Marko gulped thirstily and tried to make plans. Perhaps he could just follow the roof along its serpentine border to a set of stairs closer to his home.

There was nothing else in the guard hut except for a large, roughly square bundle in the corner. As the guard paced from window to window, Marko scooted over to inspect the package, lifting away the several thick animal skins that covered it. He hoped that whatever was hidden underneath was edible, but it was a long rope ladder.

His mind jumped back to the conversation weeks ago at his kitchen table. Spies, and wooden ladders, and his father being impressed with his suggestion, then angry about the drain near Father Anthony's house. Marko shook his head. They had used his idea, and he felt a small twinge of pride. Mama had been proud of him too. He had seen that in her face.

Mama. With enemies in the city, she would be terrified when Marko did not come home. Papa would look for him, but he would not think to look here, in a guard post. What if Commander de L'Isle retreated and forced Papa to go? He would never flee without his family. But if Marko was missing, what would he do?

Perhaps, thought Marko, finally giving in to the doubts that had plagued him for months, perhaps that was better. After all, they knew what Marko had done during that brief, unguarded moment when they had trusted him with something precious and Marko . . . Marko had failed. A glimmer of recollection danced before his eyes: dark curls, and a small voice laughing in the surf, a memory so beautiful and so excruciating that Marko squeezed his eyes shut, unable to bear the agony of examining it any further. He ignored the pleadings of his rational brain that his parents loved him no matter what—that losing him too would destroy them. "They're better off without me," he thought, and then whispered the treacherous thought out loud. "They're better off without me."

Marko was jerked from his reverie by echoing shouts that floated to him from nearby. He scrambled up in alarm. Footsteps thudded up the stone stairwell. The guard was tense, his sword held ready. Marko couldn't understand what was being shouted, but his confusion gave way to almost instant clarity. Enemy soldiers were climbing the stairs. The guard wasted no time.

He threw the rope ladder hastily out the window of the guard post, and Marko watched it uncurl like a snake down the outside of the wall. The voices grew closer, laughing. The guard grabbed Marko and pushed him toward the ladder as he secured it to thick wooden posts. "Go!" he whispered. The guard turned his back, planting his feet firmly in the stone, sword raised and shoulders set. The footsteps weren't in a hurry, but Marko was. He scurried out the stone window and over the side, where he could see the beach and the shoreline in disarray, littered with abandoned tents and a single helmet bobbing upside down in the surf. He thought about home and wondered how he would ever get back through the city gates now.

It occurred to Marko that if ever there was a time for prayer, this was it. One hand over another, he descended as quickly as he could manage. His hands were sweaty, shaking with fear. "Don't slip," he told himself firmly. He was well over halfway down the wall when he heard a shout, then the clash of swords and a gurgled groan.

Marko looked up in panic. Should he climb back up

and help? He was still undecided—when a fearsome face appeared. It was nearly night, and the turbaned soldier looking down over the wall at him held a torch in one hand and a curved sword in the other. He pointed the sword at Marko and shouted.

Marko abandoned logic. He flung his feet off the ladder rung and held on to the rope edges. He slid down the ropes, bumping over the wooden slats tied between them and burning his hands on the rough weave. As soon as he thought he was close enough to jump without breaking a limb, he let go and dropped like a stone.

He landed with a sickening thud and rolled sideways, striking the back of his head on a sharp rock. He gasped, but there was no time to waste. He dashed through the underbrush, away from the city, not knowing if he was being chased but determined to put as much distance between himself and the ladder as possible. He ran until it was so dark that he could see to run no further. He clambered under a bush and lay panting on the ground. There was no sound of pursuit. No foreign voices shouting after him.

Marko hurt all over. Cuts, scrapes, and bruises decorated his body like jewelry, but the worst was the throbbing in his head. Every second brought further drumming agony. Despite his pain, he could feel the panic fleeing his muscles, immediately replaced by bone-deep exhaustion. He knew he should try to stay conscious and keep watch, but his body had other ideas. He had no energy left to fight and sank into oblivion.

CHAPTER 7

Marko heard the rustling of leaves in the wind
and the distant sound of seabirds calling to each other. He
had rolled out from underneath the bush, and the midafternoon sun beat relentlessly on his face. He knew he was
awake because his eyes were open, but the memory of how
he had gotten there was missing. He closed his eyes, con-
centrating on the heaviness of his limbs.

His head pulsed with pain, each heartbeat striking like
a blacksmith's anvil above his neck. He carefully rotated
and flexed his arms and legs. They were sore, covered
in bruises and scrapes, but whole and unbroken. Slowly,
Marko stretched his hand to the back of his head. His
hand was sticky with blood when he drew it away.

He felt the scar over his eye, but that was the old
wound. He was reassured to feel the rough line where
the skin had already knit together in healing, and blearily

remembered his mother holding a clean cloth over his forehead after his fall from the tree. She had told him that head wounds bleed a lot, and he reached around to gently prod the gash in his skull. The injury stung but didn't feel large, and the bleeding had slowed to almost nothing.

Marko maneuvered his elbows and forced his torso upward, regretting his decision when a surge of nausea threatened to topple him. He gritted his teeth and rode the wave, one hand clasped against his head. When it had subsided, he crawled gingerly out from the tangled branches of the bush toward a small grove of trees and propped himself up against a smooth trunk in the shade. The nausea and pain frightened him. He was sure that he must have hit his head, and hard, but he couldn't remember how it had happened.

Marko allowed himself a moment to steady his breathing before forcing himself to think. Squinting against the afternoon sunlight, he looked at the unfamiliar landscape around him. He could see through the tangle of branches to the city wall in the distance, and the memories flooded back. He had jumped from the broken tree limb to the wall. The guard shack on top of the wall. The guard who had sent him out the window when the enemy approached. After that, the images were jumbled: climbing down the ladder, the terror of being discovered, letting go, the gut-wrenching emptiness of falling, and the pain of striking his head.

It had been night when he escaped. He squinted at the sun, trying to judge time by the warmth that was now heating his legs. Was it midday? He couldn't quite make his brain count the hours, but knew it was long enough for his parents to notice his absence.

His parents. Papa had been at the fort, and now the enemy army was in the city. Was he safe? Marko patted his side. He was comforted to find his knife still tucked into the loop at his belt. He was glad Mama had insisted on it.

Mama. Mama would be frantic. He fought back a visceral urge for them, the pain tangling with nausea. Gritting his teeth, Marko struggled to his feet, leaning heavily on the tree for support. He closed his eyes tightly until the world righted itself again and hobbled toward the distant wall.

In the darkness and panic last night, he had run heedlessly. Marko was surprised to see how far he had come from the city. He stumbled past broken grasses and snapped twigs, following the path of destruction he had left behind while fleeing.

He was covered with dirt and spit dust out of his mouth. The gulls he had heard still cried in the distance, but he couldn't see the ocean. He sniffed the air. The smell of salt was faint and confirmed his distance from the water.

Marko tried to form a mental map of his surroundings. He had been lost when he climbed the tree yesterday, but the brief moments on top of the battlement had gifted him with an aerial view of the city, and he had thought he knew the direction of home. But now he was on the wrong side of the wall, and everything looked the same. He half-heartedly brushed at a few large leaves clinging to his legs but gave up when the motion aggravated his already pounding head.

He was outside Rhodes. The city was occupied by an enemy force and surrounded by a wall that he had no idea how to penetrate. In the guard hut, he had been sure that his family was better off without him. That conviction had abandoned him, leaving behind fear and an empty loneliness. He wanted to go home. He thought first to make his way along the outside of the city wall to the drain near his home, but remembered with regret that he had told his father about that conduit, and it was filled and impassible.

But . . . the possibility existed that there were others. His only option was to look for one.

The shortest distance to his house would be to follow the wall around the city to the northwest, but that would take him through miles of beach occupied by foreign soldiers. He could also go the opposite direction, the long way around, away from the sea and across the open plain. Marko paled at the thought of trying to sneak through an enemy camp with a kitchen knife as his only defense, and he turned resolutely to the south. With the sea at his back, he stumbled toward home.

He kept the wall to his left and always within eyesight, but the tall grasses offered more camouflage than the beaten path at the wall's base. The heat and long summer had baked the grass to a soft brown, and for once he was thankful for his small stature, as the grass grew almost to his shoulders, brushing against his neck in the soft breeze.

Midday gave way to evening as Marko forced one foot in front of the other. His snail's pace was frustrating, but every time he tried to speed up, dizziness slowed him again. His empty stomach was also a problem. Once the nausea abated, hunger pangs took over.

Months of siege rations had given him intimate knowledge of never having enough to eat. Marko stubbornly ignored his stomach, focusing on listening for the sounds of running water. He knew from trips outside the city to visit his grandparents that several streams wound their way down from the mountains to empty in the sea near Rhodes. It was the end of August, still high summer; there would be no rain for weeks, and his only hope of water came from the ground. His lips were chapped, and he panted, his breaths keeping time with the throbbing in his head. Marko was accustomed to hunger, but the well in his yard had never lacked water.

The sun was setting when Marko stumbled across a tiny creek meandering through a small meadow. He fell to his knees and plunged his face into the cool water, drinking his fill before collapsing in a heap on the bank. He splashed the back of his neck, washing away dirt and dried blood while trying to cool himself. A rock nudged him in the ribs, and he rolled to a more comfortable position, only to find that the lump was in his shirt, not the grass. He reached inside and found the note he had been charged to deliver, wedged alongside the chunk of bread that had been meant for his father's meager supper. Marko lay his head on the grass and unwrapped the package, allowing himself three small bites before stowing it back in the hidden pocket. There was nothing to be done about the note. He stashed it next to the bread.

Fig trees grew wild along the banks of the creek, and Marko halfheartedly looked into the green foliage. He was not surprised to find the branches stripped bare. A stray wind ruffled the empty trees and tickled his nose. The late summer wildflowers rustled, a sea of red and pink and fuchsia that interrupted the endless view of grass. The air was cooler now, and Marko could smell a hint of the sea.

There was a field like this one near his grandparents'

farm, filled with flowers that bowed their bright heads in the breeze. He had lain on his belly once with Elias, their chins propped identically on their hands as they watched a grasshopper climb one of the wildflower stems. The insect had held on tightly as the stalk waved back and forth like a pendulum, until it was suddenly gone, a powerful spring of hind legs propelling it out of sight. Elias had shrieked with laughter, and Marko laughed out loud reflexively, remembering the feel of the small boy who had then climbed on his back and begged Marko to find more. Marko had complied, of course, and their father had found them there, hours later, still watching grasshoppers as Elias whooped in delight as each one jumped. Papa had swung the small boy up to carry him back to the house and thrown a companionable arm around Marko's shoulders as they walked to dinner, laughing. Marko melted under the weight of the memory; two days later had been the worst day of his life, and he thought that had been the last time that his father had touched him in happiness and warmth instead of anger.

Remembering was pain. He jerked his head, shaking

off the memory, and stood to continue walking. He had taken only two steps when he heard the sound of people. He turned toward the voices, opening his mouth to call for help when the words became clearer. Marko's elation plunged into panic, for the conversation was not in his native Greek—but in the guttural dialogue that he remembered from his encounters in the city. They were not his countrymen—but a squadron of enemy soldiers patrolling the wall.

Marko looked frantically around, searching for a place to hide. Neither the wall nor the fig trees offered refuge, but he spotted a group of boulders that marked the nearby edge of a clearing. Crouching low, he checked that his knife was still tucked firmly into his belt and made himself as small as possible. He crept behind the bushes at the creek's edge. The sounds of foreign conversation grew louder.

Marko could hear his heart beating in his ears, a drumming sound so loud that he was certain it would betray his position as he scuttled through the grasses. Struggling to keep his breath from escaping his mouth in gasps, he eased closer to his goal. Reaching the first boulder, he inched to the opposite side, placing it between himself and the approaching danger. He was sliding one foot forward to check the location of the patrol when, without warning, a hand reached from behind and clamped firmly on his mouth.

Marko struggled against the arms that wrapped around him. He managed to pull the kitchen knife from the loop on his belt and twisted, attempting to plunge the knife into his attacker's leg, but his captor's strength far outmatched his own. An arm encircled firmly around his chest, pinning his left arm to his side. Another arm grabbed his in a vise-like grip around his wrist, forcing his hand to point the knife downward and away from the assailant.

"Be still," hissed a voice in his own language. "Do not make a sound if you want to live."

CHAPTER 8

Marko froze, breathing heavily through his nose in an attempt to calm his mind and still the trembling in his limbs. The knife twitched in his hand, but he could not move it further. The muscular arm around his middle relaxed slightly but did not release him.

"I am a friend," the voice whispered in his ear. "There is a band of soldiers nearby. If they see us, they will kill us. Nod if you understand."

Marko nodded in one sharp jerk, completely consumed with fear. The arm tightened, but this time in comfort, not capture.

"Look to your right," his new friend continued in a low voice as he released his hold on Marko's mouth. "There is a path through the boulders, away from here. We can follow the city wall and look for a place to hide."

"I know a p-place," Marko whispered, panic

interrupting his speech. "It is by the sea, a c-cave hidden in the cliffs."

There was no sound as the stranger seemed to think this over. "Are you sure you can find it? It will be dark soon."

Marko nodded and heard a small sigh behind him. "It's not as though we have many other options," the voice said, as if to himself. "You had best take us there."

Marko's shoulders stiffened in surprise. Us? The arms holding him gradually released their pressure, and Marko turned. His rescuer was a man in his late thirties with warm topaz eyes and a long nose with a hump in the middle of the bridge. The rest of his face was hidden by a surprisingly tidy chestnut beard which ended well below his shoulders. He was slim and seemed to blend in to the dusky surroundings. Marko realized with a start that it was because he was clad completely in black. Marko's eyes widened as he recognized the cassock and black *skoufos* on the stranger's head, identifying him as one of the many monks on the island.

Behind him in the shadows stood a second cassock-clad

man, younger than his companion but taller, with wide shoulders and thick arms that made him look more suited to carrying giant slabs of rock than being a monastic. His head was oddly camouflaged in the darkness. He stepped forward to stand by the first monk, and the riot of black curls that hid his forehead and the lower half of his face reminded Marko of the flocks of sooty black sheep he had seen in the countryside. He had a sudden, wild thought that the man was only missing horns. At any other time, it might have been funny.

The monk's tangled, bushy beard grew out from his chin in every direction, climbing up his pale cheeks to disappear in the mop of curly spirals that fell over dark, sparkling eyes. The eyes were framed by deep laugh lines, but for now they were narrowed, watching Marko warily.

"I am Father Ignatios," the first monk said. "And this is Father Kosmas. We are from the monastery of Panagia Tsambika. Do you know where that is?"

Marko nodded. "S-south," he stuttered. Taking a deep breath, he tried again. "It is south of Rhodes, on the way to Archangelos. My Papa has visited before." He moved his shoulders, glad to be free from Father Ignatios's solid grip and wondering if he would be bruised in the morning.

Father Ignatios smiled. "Good. I may have met him, which means we are not quite strangers. What is your name?"

"Marko."

Father Ignatios held up a sudden hand in warning, and Marko was instantly still, moving only to adjust his grip on the knife he still clutched. The sound of the patrol drifted to them, and Father Ignatios nodded grimly to Father Kosmas.

"Marko. Listen carefully. The wind has changed and is carrying their voices toward us, which means they are less likely to hear us if we go now. Are you ready?" He held out a hand to Marko, and Marko put his knife away. He hesitated for a brief second before placing his fingers in the monk's firm grip. The sensation of human contact was strangely foreign, and Marko realized that he could not remember the last time he had voluntarily touched another person. Father Ignatios paused at the brief flash of emotion that dashed across Marko's face but said nothing, instead crossing himself and glancing upward.

"Let God arise! Let His enemies be scattered. Let those who hate Him flee from before His face!" He tugged gently on Marko's hand, and they inched out from behind the boulder, Father Kosmas following close behind.

Marko stayed in the shadow of the older monk, walking as close as he dared in the deep grass without stepping on the edge of his cassock. He had let go of the monk's hand, but the warmth that had been exchanged in that brief moment remained, reminding him of his mother. The day's exhaustion had been eclipsed by terror, and despite all his uncertainties and past fears, Marko suddenly wanted nothing more than to be surrounded by the close embrace of his parents.

The rapidly falling darkness helped to hide them but made their footing treacherous. Father Ignatios walked with swift steps, staying behind boulders and crouching in shadows. Marko heard a quiet breath of words around him. The monks were praying as they made their escape.

Marko measured their journey in footsteps and

breaths, each one an instant unto itself, adding up to minutes that seemed to take an eternity. They stayed as far from the soldiers as they could, but the troops roaming the area grew thicker as they neared the cliffs. Twice, Father Ignatios hissed at Marko to hide as they came upon a soldier unexpectedly. They had almost reached their destination when Marko heard the snap of a dry twig nearby.

Marko instinctively reached out to Father Ignatios, taking hold of his cassock as they sank wordlessly behind a wild vine. Father Kosmas followed them silently to the ground. Their retreat was muted by the grass at their feet, and the sudden rustling of the vine was covered by the sound of tuneless humming from the Ottoman soldier who appeared out of the darkness. They lay flat on the earth, disguised by the shadow of the city wall, as the soldier leaned against the stone boundary. He wiped a weary hand across his brow and called out in his unrecognizable tongue. Another soldier answered close behind.

Marko lay still as death. The boots of the second soldier were the only visible part of him. Marko leaned unconsciously backward; it would take only a few errant steps to be discovered, and discovery meant certain death. The two soldiers drank deeply from the waterskins hanging at their sides, laughing as one punched the other in the arm. The first soldier paused to urinate on the city wall, gesturing upward in frustration and yelling something incomprehensible. His companion laughed, and they finally stalked off to rejoin their company.

Marko let out his breath in a great gasp, realizing only then that he had been holding it and was growing light-headed. Father Ignatios helped him up. Brushing clumps of dirt off his cassock, he raised an eyebrow at Father Kosmas, who nodded his readiness. "We are nearly to the cliffs," Father Ignatios said in a low voice. "Have courage, Marko."

Marko panted, and his insides churned. Fear had overtaken him so completely that he no longer had any comprehension of what it meant not to be afraid. He looked at Father Ignatios, his eyes wide and his body shaking. The monk pulled Marko to him in a crushing embrace as his body fluttered like a leaf in the wind.

"Do you know the Fifty-fifth Psalm, Marko?"

Marko shook his head. His attendance at church had been required by his parents, but when he wasn't taking his turn as an acolyte, he had mostly passed the time watching dust float in the air. In recent months, he had flatly refused to enter a church at all.

"The psalms are a gift, and this one in particular is a great prayer in times of trouble. I will say it as we walk." Father Ignatios gripped him by the shoulders and lowered his head so his eyes were directly level with Marko's. "Can you lead us the rest of the way?"

"But the soldiers," Marko stammered. "They'll hear you."

Father Ignatios glanced around. "Do you hear the wind? It has picked up enough to cover small sounds."

Father Kosmas added in a low voice, "And most of the soldiers have been called back to report to their commanders."

"In any case," Father Ignatios said, "prayer is always worth the risk. Besides," he smiled, "I'll be quiet."

Marko nodded, taking a great gulp of air. He heard the monk begin the whispered psalm behind him as his feet found their way over terrain that was finally becoming familiar. "'Give ear to my prayer, O God, and do not despise my supplication . . .'"

They continued to walk stealthily in single file through the shadows. Marko kept one hand on the wall as they moved, the stone a solid reminder of the world outside of himself. The rest of his mind was occupied with the heartbeat he could feel in every corner of his body—pounding, pounding like a drum in his chest so hard that for a wild moment he feared his ribs would break. He forced himself to listen to Father Ignatios and ignore the swirling terror dancing at the edge of his consciousness. "'My heart was troubled within me, and the terror of death fell on me. Fear and trembling came upon me, and the darkness covered me.'"

Some dim part of Marko's brain recognized the truth in the words, and he took the smallest measure of comfort in the fact that someone else had written them; he was not the only person in the world who felt as frightened as he did at this very moment.

They left the city wall and followed the natural descent

of the land down to the water's edge. The waves rolled in and back out over the sand, providing a backdrop of sound that covered their stray footfalls and the whisper of Father Ignatios's continued prayer. The cave was near, so near, and Marko could believe, for the first time, that they might make it.

"'But I cried out to God, and the Lord heard me. Evening and morning and midday, I shall tell; I shall proclaim, and He will hear my voice,'" Father Ignatios murmured, reaching out his hand to the cliff face that suddenly loomed in front of them, steep but not vertical. Marko took the lead, following the narrow path that wound back and forth up the cliff face, hidden in places by bushes and the scraggly trees that kept some miraculous hold in the stone.

It was a dangerous trail in the daylight, and few would attempt it after sunset, but Marko had climbed this treacherous footpath nightly for months. The monks followed behind, occasionally stumbling or knocking stray rocks down the cliff face as they moved higher. Marko heard a muttered, "Lord have mercy," coming continually from the mouth of Father Kosmas, but Father Ignatios never wavered in his recitation.

They inched their way up the rocky face, Marko quietly gesturing to hidden footholds along the way, and occasionally grasping ragged plant life for support. "'Cast your care upon the Lord,'" Father Ignatios breathed, "'and He shall support you; He will never allow the righteous to be moved. But You, O God, will bring them down into the pit of decay; men of blood and deceit shall not live even half their days. . . .'"

Marko ducked through the bushes into his cave, his sudden movement causing a yelp of shock from the monk behind him as he disappeared from sight. Marko reached out blindly, grasping a handful of fabric and heaving forward, pulling an off-balance Father Ignatios face-first into the cave. The two of them landed in a heap on the dusty floor before the monk had a chance to register his near fall. Father Ignatios clenched his eyes shut in relief, and Father Kosmas joined them inside, finishing the psalm for his companion, "'But I will hope in You, O Lord.'"

CHAPTER 9

MARKO SAT WITH HIS BACK against the jagged rock of the cave wall, looking out into the darkness and hearing the sound of the sea. The wind caressed his face, and a great calm washed over him. For weeks and months, he had kept his promise to his parents and had not strayed from the city. In doing so, he had nearly forgotten how he craved the peace of this place. The relief of safety made his body limp, and although there was no solitude, he was oddly comforted by the presence of the two monks he had met in the meadow.

"Father Ignatios?" he said quietly.

"I am here, Marko." He felt the monk shift next to him. "Do you need something to eat?"

Marko heard a great rumble from his midsection at the mention of food. "I have a little bread," he said.

"Eat it, and this as well." Father Ignatios pressed a soft

roundness into his hands. Marko bit into it, discovered fruit, and ate ravenously before he could register the type. The monks passed him a skin bag of water, and he drank deeply. His hunger and thirst sated, exhaustion took hold.

Father Ignatios patted his shoulder as Marko's body relaxed next to him. "Lie down and rest, Marko. You were right; we are well hidden here. Father Kosmas and I will keep watch through the night, and we will decide what to do in the morning."

"Please don't leave," Marko said without thinking as his eyes closed. A yawn stretched his jaw, making his ears pop.

"I will not," Father Ignatios said. "For now, sleep. God is with you."

Marko opened his mouth to respond but was asleep before he could form any words.

WHEN MARKO OPENED his eyes in the morning, he was inside a cloud. Fog had drifted over the ocean in the early morning and through the mouth of his cave. He reached up tentatively with one hand and felt only emptiness, his fingers drifting through the swirling moisture with no resistance. Marko inhaled a long breath, his nose twitching slightly at a smell that did not belong in the mist but brought to mind icons and chanting.

"Good morning, Marko," Father Ignatios said from behind him.

"You smell like incense," Marko replied, scooting backward to sit next to the monks.

"Well, I am a monk," he said. "Have something to eat." He passed a small chunk of rough brown bread to Marko, who ate as slowly as he could manage, not wanting to waste a single crumb. It did not satisfy his hunger.

"Now tell us, Marko," Father Kosmas began in a tone that immediately put Marko on guard. "What were you doing outside the city on your own?"

"Traveling," answered Marko.

Father Kosmas raised his bushy black eyebrows, clearly not impressed with his answer.

"Where are your parents?"

Marko shrugged. The honest reply was that he had no idea, but somehow he didn't believe that was sufficient.

Now that yesterday's terror had passed, he found himself wondering if he truly did want to reunite with his family. The obvious answer, when he would allow himself to admit the truth, was yes. But would they want to reunite with him? Of that, Marko was less sure.

The monks waited patiently, watching the flood of thoughts and emotions war across Marko's face.

"Marko," Father Ignatios asked softly, "why are you all alone?"

The gentleness of his voice hurt, and Marko was suddenly ashamed.

"I was afraid," he admitted, looking at the cave floor between his feet. "I was taking a message to my father when the army broke into the city. I was caught up in the crowd, and got lost, and I had to go over the wall to get away from the soldiers. But I fell and hit my head, and when I woke up it was the next day. I didn't know what to do."

He looked desperately at the monks. "My father works for Commander de L'Isle, and if he retreated, he would have made Papa go with him. So I don't know where my parents are. I don't know if they're at home, or if they had to leave. I . . . I don't even know if they're alive."

Father Kosmas leaned back against the wall and eyed Marko pensively, his thick arms crossed over his chest. Father Ignatios, who was toying with the prayer rope in his hands, looked insubstantial next to the bulk of his brother monk. A long moment passed before the smaller monk nodded slightly, as if in answer to an unheard question.

"We will take you home to your parents, Marko, and then—"

Marko let out a small wounded sound before burying his face in his knees. He wanted his mother with every fiber of his being. He missed his father's steadying presence; he wished his sister was sitting next to him in quiet companionship. But battling with his fervent desires was fear, the terror that he had ruined their lives along with his own and that there was no coming back from that.

"I can't go," Marko finally croaked, his face still hidden from the monks.

Father Ignatios tilted his head to the side. "And why not?" he asked quietly.

Marko lifted his face and toyed with a loose string on the end of his shirt. The monks made no sound, waiting in patient silence for Marko to reply.

"Last year," he said haltingly, "there was a—an accident. It was my fault. I'm afraid to go home. I don't know how to be a part of my family anymore. Another bad thing might happen." There was a long, expectant pause while the monks waited for Marko to continue.

"What happened in the accident, Marko?" asked Father Kosmas.

Marko shook his head violently. Father Kosmas opened his mouth to ask again, but Father Ignatios put a hand on his arm. The monks had a murmured conference and then stood. Father Ignatios held out his hand. "Come with us," he said. Marko was unsure if it was an invitation or an order, but he allowed the monk to help him to his feet as he followed them to the mouth of the cave. Marko could hardly see the ocean through the thick fog but realized quickly as his eyes began to sting that it was not only fog, but smoke shrouding the view.

"What is burning?" he asked, the smell of smoke stinging his nostrils.

"Panagia Filerimos," Father Kosmas replied in a low voice, grief coloring his tone.

"The monastery?" Marko was shocked. "How do you know?"

"We met a family on the road yesterday who said it was on fire, but we won't know for sure until we meet Father Nestor. He went ahead to investigate."

Father Ignatios looked at Marko. "Father Nestor is our abbot. We ran out of food and were traveling to Panagia Filerimos to stay with the monks there. But once we heard about the fires, we didn't know if it was safe to continue. Father Nestor went ahead to see. We were supposed to meet him last night, but we ran into the patrol."

"And you," added Father Kosmas.

"And you," the older monk agreed. "We had a second plan in case we were unable to find him last night, so we will try again today. He will be waiting west of here, a few miles away. If we can avoid any more soldiers, I think we will find him in a few hours." As he spoke, a sudden breeze stirred against their faces. The smoke mingled with fog swirled, lifting enough that Marko could see the ocean waves breaking on the rocks below and the narrow path that they had traversed the night before.

Father Ignatios groaned softly as he peered over Marko's shoulder at the treacherous drop and steep slope. He took an involuntary step back. Father Kosmas noticed the movement and glanced to see what he was looking at. "Looks different in the light, doesn't it?" He nudged Father Ignatios with his elbow, knocking the slight man backward a step, a teasing grin lighting up his ruddy face.

Father Ignatios shuddered. "Don't remind me. Following that path in the dark was one of the most terrifying things I've ever done."

"Our Father Ignatios is afraid of heights," Father Kosmas informed Marko with a glint in his dark eyes.

Marko glanced at Father Ignatios in surprise. The monk's face had paled as he looked back over the precipitous trail. Father Ignatios saw Marko's look of surprise. "Why do you think I was praying so fervently?"

"I thought you were praying for me to be brave," Marko said.

"Oh yes, that too," Father Ignatios replied. "But being brave myself was first on my mind."

"Not to interrupt your joyful recollections"—Father Kosmas stretched his massive arms over his head and pointed out of the cave—"but that path is our only way down. I'd like to try it in the daylight this time."

Father Ignatios swallowed hard and crossed himself. "Back we go," he said grimly. "Shall we say the same prayer on the climb down?"

The sun shone high overhead when the small band met the abbot that afternoon in a copse of trees that hid them from the sight of enemy patrols. Marko rubbed his sore legs. They had walked for hours, the city disappearing into the distance as they traveled. Soldiers patrolled the road, so they stuck to the trees and fields out of sight, ducking and hiding at times when horses paraded past. Uneven terrain and having to hide had added hours to their day.

"God be praised, you're safe!" Father Nestor embraced his two monks, throwing one arm around each of them and holding them in a tight embrace. "With all the patrols, when you missed our meeting last night, I was frightened." Father Nestor was older than the other monks but several inches shorter than Father Ignatios. He was completely dwarfed by the bulk of Father Kosmas, but then, reflected Marko, everyone was smaller than Father Kosmas. The abbot's face was leathery and lined, with the tanned, weather-beaten look of someone who had spent most of his long life outdoors.

"Panagia Filerimos is safe," Father Nestor told his fellow monks, and Father Ignatios crossed himself and muttered a brief prayer of thanksgiving. "The fire is in a field nearby. I think it started by accident. But soldiers were using the monastery well to put it out, and they're raiding the church."

Father Kosmas made a growling noise deep in his throat. "And the monks? Are they hurt?"

Father Nestor shook his head, his tangled black and silver hairs shaking violently. "I think they escaped, God be praised. And they would not have left without protecting the valuables, but that church houses ancient icons as well. God alone knows what the marauders will steal or destroy." He sighed and looked past Father Ignatios. His gray eyebrows leaped up into his forehead as he registered Marko's presence.

"This is Marko," Father Ignatios said. "We came across him on our way here. He was forced over the city wall during the fighting. He helped us hide last night, and we brought him with us."

Father Nestor exhaled loudly and looked at Marko with a piercing gaze. Marko squirmed. "Well, now. This changes things. A lone boy trying to sneak back into the city could easily be killed by soldiers who will not bother to ask questions." He glanced at Father Ignatios. "Do you think we can make it safely back to the city?"

Father Ignatios nodded. "We saw a few patrols on our way here, but as long as we stay off the roads, I think we will be hidden."

The abbot nodded his head decisively. "Then Marko, we will see you back safely to your parents and then continue on to Panagia Filerimos."

"I don't . . ." Marko began, but swallowed his

argument at the sight of the extreme disapproval written on Father Nestor's face. The abbot blinked and reached to Marko. The fingers on his hand were twisted, curled, and locked into loose fists, pointing in unnatural directions. Marko stared at them.

"Forgive me, Marko," the older monk said quietly. "In the monastery, one of the greatest things that is asked of us is obedience. But I forgot for a moment that you are not a monk." He paused and waited for Marko to meet his eyes, bright and piercing. "Will you give me your trust, Marko, and stay with us for your own safety? Will you trust me to do all that is within my power to return you to your family?"

Marko cleared his throat and looked at Father Ignatios with pleading eyes. Father Ignatios whispered a few sentences quietly into the abbot's ear, and Father Nestor studied him for a long moment, his long, bushy eyebrows wagging slightly in the breeze, like wobbly insect antennae. His hazel eyes were filled with appraisal and understanding. "It seems we have more to discuss," Father Nestor finally said. "But for now, you will be safe with us."

Marko was raw, filled with indecision and fright. He didn't know what else to do, what else he could do, so he nodded his assent. Father Nestor rested one of his twisted hands gently on Marko's back. Marko flinched but took a deep breath and forced himself to relax.

"I know you are afraid," Father Nestor said gently. "We all are. But we must remember the words of Saint Anthony: 'Even the devil is afraid when we pray. He runs away when we make the sign of the cross.' So cross yourself, Marko, gather your courage, and stay close."

The three monks and their young charge made an abrupt turn in the direction from which they had come. A long, twisting walk through the underbrush lay ahead of them. Marko groaned under his breath. He could picture every hill, wood, and stream bed they had just traversed, and he dreaded the long trek back to the city. The monks were undeterred, and he fell reluctantly in line behind them.

A TWO HOUR RETURN JOURNEY on the dusty road brought them to the edge of a field. Father Nestor pointed ahead with a curled finger. "Look."

Marko shaded his eyes against the sun and followed the line of the monk's outstretched arm. A dusty footpath wove through the grasses and ended at a trio of stone buildings in the distance: a house with a nearby barn and shed.

"Do you think they will have food?" Marko asked desperately.

Father Nestor frowned, his eyes focused on the distant farm. "Nobody has very much of anything these days, Marko. But God willing, we will find something."

Marko closed his eyes tightly and tried to think of something else.

"Soldiers!" whispered Father Kosmas.

Marko's eyes flew open in panic. "Where? Are they ours?"

"No," Father Kosmas said. "Marko, forgive me. They are still in the distance. Do you see them down the road?"

Marko saw the band of soldiers rounding a bend. They were mounted on horses and held long poles with brightly colored pennants that snapped in the breeze.

"Their banner says they are part of Suleiman's personal guard," Father Kosmas said. The wind whipped his copious dark curls into his face, and he grabbed a handful of hair and yanked it back, pulling the mass into a tight bunch and tying a leather strap around it with practiced ease. They left the road and ducked into a field.

"You can read their language?" Marko asked warily.

Father Kosmas was unoffended by his suspicion and brushed the twist of hair back over his shoulder. "I spent much of my youth working for the harbormaster in Kos. People from all over docked there. I learned many languages."

"How did you end up in Kos?" Marko asked.

"That's a story for another time. Quickly and quietly

now," Father Kosmas said, pointing toward a rocky path. They were forced to carefully choose each step as they navigated the almost invisible trail.

Marko fell into step close to Father Ignatios, whose stomach made a sudden growl. Marko's own stomach answered, and he tucked his head in embarrassment. He was hungry, but Father Ignatios was hungrier. They had eaten Marko's last meager lump of bread before leaving the cave, but Father Ignatios had been so sick with fright from the descent that he had vomited up his portion as soon as they reached the sea.

Father Ignatios saw him squirm and waved his hand casually in the air. "It's going to be fine, Marko. When we get to the farm, perhaps they will have something to settle our stomachs." He chuckled ruefully, though his face was wan. "I'm still not sure how we made that climb in the dark."

"The grace of God," Father Kosmas said firmly, a few steps behind them. "As St. Paul said, 'I can do all things through Christ who strengthens me.'"

"Have you always been fearful of heights?" Marko asked Father Ignatios.

"No," he replied thoughtfully, his golden eyes clouding with memory. "When I was young, I took a dare to climb into the bell tower of the church in the village where I grew up. My best friend went with me. While we were climbing, it started to rain, and Stavros—my friend—he slipped. The fall broke his neck, killing him instantly. Since then, I have never had the heart, or the stomach, for heights."

A deep chasm yawned open in Marko, and he stumbled on a stray rock. Father Ignatios looked at him curiously. Marko cast about in his mind for a distraction, a change of subject—anything to avoid further talk of accidents and death. "How did your monastery get its name?" he finally asked.

"Oh, that's a great story," replied Father Kosmas cheerfully as he caught up but completely missed the undercurrent of the conversation. Marko walked in his shadow, watching the monk's curly head twist and turn, looking in every direction. He reminded Marko of a large, inquisitive animal, always on the lookout for new smells and adventures.

Father Nestor walked at the back of the group, keeping watch as the road disappeared behind them. He made a shushing noise at his young monk, sternly jerking his head toward the soldiers still visible in the distance, but there was a fondness in his voice that made Marko's heart skip. His father used to make that noise at him. Father Kosmas instantly obeyed his elder and lowered his voice but continued his story. "Years ago, a shepherd was caring for his flock and saw a strange light. It looked like a vigil lamp, but there was no one else nearby. He followed the light to the top of a hill and saw it coming from inside a cypress tree."

"Inside of the tree?" Marko murmured, hoping that if he focused completely on what Father Kosmas was saying, Father Ignatios would lose interest in their conversation and ask no questions.

Father Kosmas nodded, his whole body bouncing as he walked. "Inside the tree! The shepherd looked, and there was an icon of the Theotokos hidden deep within the trunk. He took it out and brought it to the priest of his church, but the next day it had gone missing. Another shepherd saw the light again and found the icon back inside the same cypress tree."

"Who put it there?" Marko asked woodenly. He risked a glance at Father Ignatios and found the monk studying him intently, concern written across his features.

Father Kosmas smiled and clapped his hands together. He ducked his head and shot a guilty look at his abbot, who sighed at the noise and stared pointedly down his long nose. "Kosmas. Quietly."

"Father, forgive me," the monk said humbly. He turned back to Marko and with a significantly lower voice, said, "It was the Panagia! It happened three times—they pulled the icon from the tree and took it to the church, but the next day, the icon was back inside the tree. The priest finally said that the Panagia must want her icon to be on that hilltop, so a church was built there to house it, and eventually a monastery called Panagia Tsambika— Theotokos of the Spark."

"And you're still afraid of heights?" Marko asked Father Ignatios without thinking.

"I am," Father Ignatios replied quietly. "We all must

take our turn walking through the valley of the shadow of death, Marko. All we can do is pray for peace and the courage to endure the passage. For God is with us."

Father Nestor stepped between them and held up his twisted hand, shepherding his small flock further through the camouflage of the tall grass. The winding path led them along the edge of the field, and he brushed a low-hanging branch out of the way with the back of his hand. Marko glanced at the contorted fingers, his gaze returning to them over and over as he stumbled after the elder. Several knuckles were swollen and red, frozen at unnatural angles. Marko looked at his own hands, wondering how Father Nestor could hold anything or even feed himself. He closed his fingers tightly.

Father Nestor, who apparently missed nothing, quirked a small smile at Marko. "They don't hurt." He held out his hands for Marko to see clearly. "Part of the conditions of growing old." A muffled shout caught his attention, and the older monk squinted back at the road, his long eyebrows wiggling. Maybe his eyebrows weren't like antennae, Marko mused. Caterpillars perhaps. "Quietly now,"

Father Nestor said. "The patrol is still nearby."

The sun passed its zenith high overhead, and the light melted from the stark brightness of midafternoon into the softer glow of early evening. The foothills that flanked the stone farmhouse were bathed in hazy sunlight when Father Kosmas knocked on the door. The farmer was a large, burly man with hair that almost rivaled the curls of Father Kosmas. He refused the monks' quiet request for food and was about to drive them off when his mother, a tiny woman bent nearly double with age, pulled him down by his ear and hissed threats into his face.

The family had a single goat, a scrawny, pathetic animal that was nearly as hungry as the people who drank her milk. The farmer's cheeks burned with shame as he poured half of the goat's milk into an earthenware cup. He handed it silently to Father Nestor.

Marko had two deep swallows as his share, and he consumed it with gratefulness, licking his top lip to ensure he swallowed every drop. The monks drank their portions quietly, and Father Nestor blessed the family, offering the monks' prayers for the household's welfare.

The little grandmother hobbled after them as they left the house, speaking nonstop as she berated her son for daring to refuse to share with God's monastics—and a child that they had with them too! How in the world had that happened? Was he a young novice? Oh, clearly not, because, where was his cassock? A younger brother perhaps? Oh, what a world this was with invaders and who knew what else. It looked like none of them had eaten in weeks, and wasn't it just like her son to be selfish and bring down God's wrath on them for not sharing what little they had? She had half a mind to box his ears like he was a young lad and remind him to be thankful. She was still chattering when she eventually turned back to the house.

Marko was thankful for the milk, but it had not been enough. In any other time, there would be wild fruit, rabbits and field mice scurrying through the vegetation, and kind farmers sharing their bounty with travelers along the way. But the countryside was utterly barren; the rows of olive trees and grape arbors were empty, all the wild creatures had been hunted down. The air was eerily quiet, absent of the calling of birds and the buzzing of insects.

They followed the ancient footpath after leaving the farm, Father Nestor unwilling to return to the road and risk running into soldiers. Father Kosmas, his boundless energy undeterred by hunger, continually left the path to explore small fields and wooded groves. His bushy head broke through the trees nearby, and he beckoned them joyfully. They found him proudly pointing at a walnut tree that was growing in the woods.

Marko joined the monks in scouring the grass under the leafy boughs. His grandparents had walnuts; every summer he would spend a day with his cousins picking the fallen nuts after the men had carefully shaken the trees. He deftly separated the ripe, pale yellow-green spheres from those that were blackened and cracked or had been chewed by animals. He discarded the rotten nuts and piled the edible treasure in a growing mound to the side of the tree. When Marko could find no more, he stood to contemplate the tree growing above him.

Papa and the other men had always stood a short distance away and shaken the trees with ropes tied around the branches. Marko had no rope, but he had hands. He walked to the base of the tree, grasping a rough, low-hanging branch. Father Nestor shouted, "Marko, don't!" But it was too late, and Marko shook the tree with all his strength.

Nuts rained down around him, and Marko looked at Father Nestor in confusion. "What's the matter?"

Father Nestor opened his mouth to answer when Marko felt the first sting. Then the second. And suddenly, his neck and back and scalp were on fire as he was bitten mercilessly by whatever insects had fallen along with the walnuts.

Marko howled, beating his shoulders and arms with his fists and frantically scratching his head in an attempt to kill the tiny beasts that were down his shirt and caught in his hair. Father Kosmas grabbed his arm and hauled him away, but Marko paid no attention as he continued his losing battle against his invisible tormenters.

"Hold still," Father Kosmas bellowed as he ripped Marko's shirt up over his head and pushed him into a nearby stream. Marko thrashed, but Father Kosmas held him down, the water washing away scores of red ants. The monk let go of his arms only to tip Marko's head back and attempt to drown the creatures left in his hair.

When every last ant was washed away, Marko gingerly climbed out of the stream. Father Kosmas had thrown his shirt in the water as well, and Marko fished it out and rinsed it thoroughly, glaring at the stray ants that washed out of the fabric. He turned and silently walked back through the woods after Father Kosmas, sopping wet and itchy.

Father Nestor was stomping on the pile of ripe walnuts that they had gathered, a safe distance from the tree that was visibly teeming with a multitude of ants climbing back up the trunk to their nest somewhere in the canopy. Father Ignatios knelt at the edge of the pile, separating the nuts from the cracked rinds, his hands colored a sickly green from the outer shells. The two monks looked up at Marko, and he saw Father Ignatios's hazel eyes twitch briefly at the sight of him standing there dripping.

Father Nestor shook his silvery head. "I'm sorry, Marko," he said. "That happened to me as a boy, and I've been wary of nut trees ever since. The bites are brutal but not poisonous. You're in for a long night, but you'll survive."

Marko scratched his neck, and suddenly every one of his bites—it felt like there were hundreds—caught fire, and he began to wildly scratch his entire torso. Father Nestor stood and removed his worn cassock, deftly wrapping it around Marko. It fell in a pile around his feet, but Father Nestor expertly pulled and tucked, and his stiff fingers finally tied the cassock around Marko's waist. "Head behind a tree and get out of the rest of your wet clothes," the older monk ordered. "You can lay them out on rocks to dry and wear this for now." Father Nestor returned to stomping, looking oddly like Marko's grandfather in the simple pants and shirt he wore under the cassock, his salt-and-pepper beard reaching the middle of his chest.

Marko quickly scrambled out of the rest of his wet garments, beating his shirt against a boulder for good measure before laying all of his clothes out to dry. Something white fluttered to the ground. It was the letter he had been directed to deliver to his father. He carefully pressed the water off the thick paper and laid it on the boulder, weighing it down with a rock.

He sat scratching his bites until Father Ignatios sent him to the stream to wash the nuts he had extracted. Marko gathered them in the pockets of Father Nestor's cassock and washed the hulls carefully. Once rinsed clean of the pith that had surrounded them, the walnuts were the same familiar wrinkly brown shape that he remembered from helping Mama. They would work together, laying the washed walnuts on cloths to dry in the sun. Marko gathered the nuts, carried them carefully back to the monks, and laid them on a platter of clean leaves that Father Kosmas had prepared.

The sun had disappeared into the west, and the small clearing was dusky. Father Kosmas ducked back to the road to check for soldiers. Reporting none in sight, he lit a small fire in the protected covering of several thick tree trunks, and the blaze danced cheerfully. Father Ignatios found several large, flat rocks and some hand-sized round stones. He, Father Kosmas, and Marko sat in the small circle of firelight, smashing the clean walnuts with the stones on the flat rocks, releasing the soft, nutty interior. Father Nestor's hands would not hold a rock, so he busied himself exploring the surrounding woods. The darkness did not allow him to go far, but as the stars winked awake and the nearly full moon rose, the darkness became less impenetrable and complete.

"This would be easier if they had dried out in the sun for a few days," Father Ignatios commented as he banged relentlessly with his stone, but Marko didn't care. He was hungry now. He ate the insides of the first dozen nuts that he smashed without hesitation. The flesh was softer than he was used to and had a gentler flavor. He supposed because the nuts were fresh and not dried, but it didn't matter. It was food.

Once his belly was no longer crying out for attention, Marko was able to focus on what he was doing. There was a trick to breaking open the tough shells; instead of smashing hard with the rock, he learned to knock it briskly on all sides with his stone until it cracked. He could then pry the nut open and tap out the insides. It became a sort of contest with himself as he tried to keep the curved shape of the nut intact.

Father Nestor emerged from the trees with a handful

of wild mint and some oddly shaped mushrooms. He beckoned to Father Kosmas, and they disappeared again. When they returned, Father Kosmas was grinning and carrying a large chunk of honeycomb, oozing with sunshine-colored honey that sparkled in the firelight.

"How did you get that without getting stung?" Marko asked.

Father Kosmas shrugged. "Bees never sting me." He licked a drip of honey that ran down his hand. "It must be my sweet demeanor."

They ate the mushrooms and handfuls of the nuts for dinner, washed down by cold, fresh water from the stream. They had no kettle to boil water for tea, but Marko crushed the mint leaves between his teeth to release the fresh, spicy flavor. He bit into a piece of the honeycomb and sighed blissfully, sucking the sweet, sticky honey and holding it in his mouth to savor it. He spit out the leftover wax and crammed the rest of the comb in his mouth. It was the closest thing to dessert Marko had had in months.

Father Nestor cautioned against eating too many of the nuts, fearing they would all have indigestion, and Marko reluctantly obeyed the abbot's wise words. He filled the monks' traveling bags with more nuts, carefully checking for bugs before packing them to the brim.

The fire burned low, but the summer air was warm, and they did not refuel it. Marko lay back, curled in the depths of Father Nestor's cassock, which smelled faintly of incense, and watched the embers. His own clothes would be dry soon, but there was a strange comfort in wrapping the older monk's garment tightly around himself. He wondered vaguely if Father Nestor had perhaps realized this when he mentioned offhand that Marko should leave his clothes to continue to dry and could remain bundled in his cassock for the night.

The soft moss of the forest floor cushioned his head, and he wiggled slightly, searching for the most comfortable position. He found it quickly and lay mostly still, his hands occasionally succumbing to scratching fits as he watched the stars flicker in the dark canopy above. The monks prayed vespers from memory, and Marko did not realize that he had dozed off until he blearily registered hearing his name.

"... Marko?" Father Nestor said.

"I do not know, Father," Father Ignatios replied in a low voice. "He is wounded and hurting. I told him today about the accident with Stavros when I was a child, and the look on his face was that of a cornered animal. He has told us nothing about himself, only that there was some kind of accident, and he says he can't bear to be a part of his family anymore."

Marko remained still and watched the monks through half-open eyes. He was not nearly awake enough to join the conversation, and some sleepy corner of his mind debated the wisdom of sharing any more of his own story anyway.

Father Nestor stroked his flyaway black and silver beard. "And you found him by the city?"

Father Ignatios nodded.

"And he told you he was lost." Father Nestor sighed. "Well, nothing has changed. We will take Marko to Rhodes. If we can find his family, he belongs with them, accident or no accident." He stretched his shoulders back and groaned softly. "As it is, we have no other clear route before us. If the army is in the city, as Marko says, all of the island has likely fallen, and we may not even be able to safely return home. All things happen for a reason; God has put Marko in front of us. We will see him safe and trust that God will guide our path from there."

"Something about Marko's story is very wrong, Father," Father Ignatios warned.

"Yes," Father Nestor agreed quietly. "Only time will answer our questions. Now, I will keep watch first and wake you, Kosmas, in three hours. Tomorrow at first light we head back to the city."

"How will we get in?" asked Father Kosmas.

Father Nestor did not open his eyes. "'All things work together for good to those who love God, to those who are called according to His purpose.'" He shrugged and sighed. "Rest for now, brothers."

Father Ignatios stood and saw Marko's open eyes, but Marko had no apology. He squirmed into a comfortable position and fell deeply asleep to the sound of Father Nestor's murmured prayers.

CHAPTER 11

THEY WOKE WITH THE SUN, the monks stretching their arms high above their heads and gathering together to quietly chant morning prayers. Marko was in a foul mood, his sleep having been interrupted by the itching and burning of his myriad ant bites. He stomped around a tree for privacy to change back into his own clothes, returning Father Nestor's cassock with a frown as he scratched his neck.

Father Ignatios placed his own calloused hand gently on top of Marko's, lifting the scratching fingers away and replacing them with a scrap of fabric that he had dipped in the stream. The cool water soothed Marko's skin and his temper, and he thanked the monk quietly.

They continued their journey to Rhodes. Marko had made a half-hearted attempt over breakfast at campaigning to return to the city on his own. Father Nestor had firmly denied his request, and he left Marko no time or space to argue. Besides, arguing would have meant explaining, and Marko could think of nothing he would enjoy less than informing the three monks of his long list of personal failings. He trudged along, placing one foot in front of the other as the familiar road passed beneath him.

Marko's belly was full enough that it didn't require much attention, which left room for his mind to wander. What would his parents say when they saw him? Would they be happy or angry? Marko wondered if his mother had cried when he hadn't come home. If she had, were they silent tears or the screaming agony he had witnessed last summer?

Marko's rambling thoughts were interrupted by unfamiliar voices nearby, and he was startled to see that they were no longer alone on the road. Several small groups of people were traveling as well. They looked to be families, mothers holding tightly to the hands of their small children, and others, around his age, huddled nearby. The travelers were headed in their same direction toward Rhodes, with sacks over their shoulders and tied to their backs. One enterprising teen was pushing a small wheel-barrow heaped with possessions. A single scraggly chicken perched on top of the pile, ruffling its feathers in the wind and reminding Marko painfully of Irene.

One oddly shaped young girl caught his eye. Upon closer inspection, Marko could see that she was wearing what appeared to be her entire wardrobe at once—several dresses, blouses, and skirts layered on top of each other and giving her a strangely round shape. She walked stiffly, her arms held straight, restricted by the many layers of fabric. She glared at Marko, lifting her chin in stubborn invitation, and he realized he was staring.

Father Nestor was deep in conversation with two men. Marko stepped aside to wait nearby, Fathers Kosmas and Ignatios with him. They watched the ragged parade of families plodding by. The older monk finished his con-ference and offered a brief blessing to each of the men in turn. They kissed his hand, taking care not to jostle the twisted fingers, then jogged to catch up with their families on the road.

"The garrison has fallen," Father Nestor said grimly.

"The sultan offered Commander de L'Isle the lives of the citizens, plus peace and food, in exchange for surrender. He said otherwise, he would storm the city and kill everyone. The commander accepted. The sultan is keeping his word and has set aside fifty of his own warships to evacuate anyone who wants to go. They are even allowed to take their valuables. The people have one day left to decide—stay or go."

"And those who stay?" Father Kosmas asked.

"They will no longer be Greek citizens, but citizens under the sultan. They may keep their land and farms but will be subject to new laws and governance."

The monks looked at each other in amazement. Marko's fear squeezed his throat shut, and he fought for breath. Where was his family? His heartbeat echoed in his ears, and he could hear nothing else. He looked up after he had regained some kind of control and found the monks watching him carefully. He jerked his head, shaking loose his current thoughts as though dislodging a buzzing insect.

Father Nestor nodded toward the people on the road. "They are all hoping for space on the ships. We will go with them for now. Since there are so many people reentering the city, we shouldn't have too much trouble. From there we will try to find Marko's parents."

Marko groaned inwardly, trying hard to keep his features expressionless as he followed the monks back onto the road. Nausea and panic rose in his throat, burning his insides with liquid anxiety. They rounded a corner, and Marko lifted his gaze from the path. An unexpected surge of terror engulfed him at the sight of the familiar city wall. His pace faltered, and he dropped behind the monks as they continued doggedly toward the city. Father Ignatios noticed his reluctance and reached out a hand, but Marko shook it off. Concern flooded Father Ignatios's gentle features, and he matched Marko's pace in silence.

The monks moved closely together, surrounding Marko with the swishing black of their cassocks as they reentered Rhodes. Ottoman soldiers flanked the gate and watched carefully as they passed. A guard shouted, and Marko froze in place as he pointed in their direction, but the soldier stalked past him, relieving a nearby traveler of the long knife that hung at his side. "No weapons," he uttered in heavily accented Greek. He returned to his post and tossed the knife aside onto a growing pile of confiscated weaponry. Marko's own hidden kitchen knife weighed heavily, but he kept his eyes straight ahead, and they passed through the gate, under the stone wall, and into the city.

There was noise all around him, but it was not the usual sounds. Marko could not quite make sense of the difference until he realized that there were no hooves on cobblestones, no animals braying in their pens or roosters crowing. He could hear no animals at all—only people, their faces pinched in hunger and their tense voices murmuring. He realized with a start that the animals must all have been eaten during the siege, and he spared a brief, agonized thought for his own small herd of goats.

The monks looked suddenly wary. Marko thought maybe they were sensing the same strange current of fear running through the surrounding crowd. Father Nestor had a silent conversation with the other monks, full of dark looks and raised eyebrows. Marko's panic rose.

The gate they had passed through was unknown to

him. He felt a familiar dread, a twisting knot of snakes that writhed in his belly. The last time he had been in a strange part of the city, he had stumbled on a battle and been driven over the wall.

Marko tripped over a loose rock in the road and fell to his knees. Father Kosmas grasped his elbow and hauled him to his feet. Marko felt a trickle of blood run down his leg and would have ignored it, but Father Nestor spotted the injury through the new rip in his pants. The abbot looked over his shoulder, and his bright eyes lit up. "Here." He pointed to a small church set back off the road. "Let us stop here to clean your leg."

The elder monk led them up a cobblestone path and to a small well in the corner of the churchyard. He pulled a bucket of fresh, cool water from the depths, and Marko splashed away the blood and grime from his knee. The wooden well cover was warped, and Father Ignatios struggled to close it. Father Nestor reached out and twisted the lid efficiently, and it fell into place with a protesting squeak. "How did you do that?" asked Marko.

Father Nestor smiled. "I know this church."

They were startled from their conversation by the voices of invaders. Marko instantly dropped into the grass. The monks followed suit, and Father Kosmas crept along the church wall to spy on what was happening. He motioned his companions forward, and the four of them took shelter behind several large bushes.

Three soldiers stood in the rear courtyard, standing over a pile of discarded frames and splintered wood. A shout came from inside the church, and the soldiers stepped back as another frame flew out a window and landed with a loud crash. The frame landed face up, and Marko saw that it was not art, or trash, but an icon. He looked more closely at the pile. They were all icons. Father Ignatios realized this too and moaned.

Marko pressed himself flat against the ground and closed his eyes, willing himself to be invisible from the wandering eyes of the marauders. He focused on the barely audible prayers of the monks surrounding him as they watched the rest of the regiment exit the church and stand arguing in the courtyard.

"The soldiers say there is nothing of value inside,"

Father Kosmas translated in a low voice. "One says that the gold is all missing, and the other says that the art is so decayed that it is not worth transporting."

"Look!" Marko breathed. "They're leaving!"

The soldiers stomped out of the churchyard in loose formation and retreated down the street. Marko allowed himself to breathe freely again. "Are they gone?"

Father Nestor nodded grimly. "But what have they done to the church?" He hastened in through a side door. Father Kosmas and Father Ignatios hurried after him.

Marko didn't follow. Now that they were in the city, he wanted to run home. He didn't want to be in the church and wanted even less to be left alone in the churchyard. Worse, he had no desire to navigate the city streets alone with enemy patrols on every corner. He groaned and forced his reluctant feet to follow the monks inside.

Daylight struggled to illuminate the nave through the few windows. Even in the dimness, Marko could see that this was a very old church. He had grown up attending Agia Irini, where the white walls and high arches lent a feeling of airy brightness to the whole place. Here, the ceilings were low, and the icons were dark from smoke and faded with age, many with patches of bare wood where paint had worn off with time and veneration. The ornately carved iconostasis was lovingly polished and shone in the few rays of light, contrasting sharply with the plain stone floors. Marko looked at the dome overhead and saw in the shadows the massive chandelier that would be filled with candles and lit on feast days.

The monks wandered through the nave, murmuring quietly to one another as they crossed themselves and bowed, venerating the large icons of Christ and the Theotokos that flanked the altar. The soldiers had pulled the individual icons off the walls, tossing them into the heap outside. The only icons that survived the brutal treatment were the four on the iconostasis, painted directly onto the wood and impossible to remove without dismantling the entire structure.

Satisfied that everything inside was safe, the monks returned to the courtyard. Father Ignatios wept softly as he surveyed the desecration. He and Father Kosmas worked in the bright sunlight without speaking, carefully returning each icon to the nave, wiping them clean of dirt and grass, and propping them on the floor against the cold stone walls.

The monks did not ask for Marko's assistance. He stood helplessly nearby and watched them work. Like the iconostasis, these icons were in poor condition and dark with age. Marko could barely make out the faces and backgrounds in most of them, and he was not surprised that the soldiers had found them worthless.

Father Kosmas lifted another icon. "Oh!" he exclaimed in surprise. "Ignatios, look!"

Father Ignatios added his own soft exclamation, and Marko moved to their side and stared. The vivid afternoon sun warmed the gold background of the icon Father Kosmas had uncovered. In the midst of its dark and broken brothers, it shone like a precious gem. "This icon looks like it was finished yesterday!" exclaimed Father Ignatios.

Father Nestor joined them, and they examined the treasure they had unearthed.

"Saint Phanourios." Marko read the inscription on the icon. His forehead creased in confusion. "Who is Saint Phanourios?"

CHAPTER 12

Father Nestor broke the silence. "I've never heard of a Saint Phanourios. Are you sure that is what it says?"

Marko pointed at the lettering and stepped aside to give Father Nestor room. A stray flicker of sun glanced across him, and the gray hairs that peppered his head shone brightly silver. "Hmm," the monk said to himself as he studied the icon closely.

The gold leaf of the background caught the rays of the dying daylight and glowed warmly like a coal in the depths of a fire. Every other icon was old, ancient even, but this one radiated newness in a way that Marko couldn't explain. He reached out a hand without thinking, drawn magnetically to the mysterious saint whose brutal demise was depicted in a series of smaller scenes around the border. He lifted the icon from Father Kosmas's hands without asking, aware suddenly of Father Ignatios's quick intake of breath and Father Nestor's thoughtful gaze. He ignored them completely, fixated on the heavy weight in his hands.

"How did the soldiers miss it?" Father Kosmas asked quietly. His exuberant energy was stilled. "They said all the icons were too old and damaged to be bothered with. Clearly they did not see this, or they would have taken it for its gold alone."

Father Nestor had not taken his eyes off of Marko, but he answered quietly, "We do not know the ways of God, my son. It could be that they were in a hurry, or it could be that God shielded it from their eyes. It is enough, like any of the mysteries of the Church, to simply know that it happened."

"And if they return?" Father Ignatios glanced down the street, as if to reassure himself that the battalion had not turned in the road.

Marko looked up from his careful study of the icon to find that Father Nestor was still watching him.

"Marko, see if you can find a clean cloth for us to wrap it with," he said.

Marko carried the icon into the church and set it carefully with the others. He poked through cupboards and baskets while the monks finished rescuing the last of the icons outside, then canvased the church for other valuables the soldiers may have missed.

After unearthing an old, torn cassock hanging in the narthex, Marko found Father Kosmas and Father Ignatios deep in discussion while leaning over a gaping hole in the floor next to the altar. He peeked around the iconostasis, unconsciously gnawing on a fingernail, and watched Father Nestor's head appear out of the hole briefly before ducking back down out of sight.

Father Ignatios saw Marko through the deacon's door and motioned him forward. Marko hesitated, strongly remembering a stern lecture from his childhood priest Father Matthias about entering the altar without permission. Father Ignatios, looking faintly impressed by his hesitation, nodded in understanding and called down the ladder, "Father Nestor, may Marko have a blessing to enter the altar?"

In the dim light, Marko saw a gnarled hand reach

up past the edge of the hole and bless haphazardly in his direction.

Marko crossed himself uneasily, feeling immensely out of place. Father Ignatios had a hurried conversation with Father Nestor then lit a small lamp from the preparation table. He lay on his belly, stretching into the pit to hand the lamp carefully to Father Nestor, who cupped it in both hands and set it gently on a shelf.

The faint light illumined a roughly square pit about seven feet deep with a ladder down one side. The walls were earth with several shelves carved out of the sides. Marko saw two gold chalices and several other liturgical items lining the ledge.

"Father Nestor was the priest here before joining us at our monastery. This is the church where he was ordained," explained Father Kosmas. "He dug this as a hiding place in case of invasion, where they could leave the church's valuables if they had to evacuate in a hurry."

Marko stepped back as Father Nestor awkwardly climbed up to join them, wrapping his wrists around the sides of the ladder to steady himself. He removed a small

bottle and a golden box from the deep pockets of his cassock, handing them gently to Father Ignatios. "I have the Chrism and the reserve Sacrament, but I do not think we can take anything else without it being discovered. The clergy must have fled in a hurry, or they would have taken these themselves."

Father Ignatios nodded. "I will write a note to leave in their place, in case they return."

"Marko, could you find me some string? Something very sturdy," called Father Kosmas.

After a brief search, Marko found a neat ball of twine stored in the chanter stand. Father Kosmas wrapped it tightly around the neck of the bottle and venerated it reverently. He hung the bottle around his neck like a cross and tucked it under his cassock, next to his heart.

Father Ignatios opened the golden box, and Marko saw several dried, bite-sized pieces of bread inside. Father Kosmas handed the other monk a small red cloth that was used to cover the chalice before Communion, and Father Ignatios carefully placed the bread inside before wrapping the cloth around it and securing the whole package with twine. He made a necklace like Father Kosmas and handed it to Father Nestor, who hung it around his neck, hidden from view. Marko watched the entire strange proceeding in bewilderment.

"This is the reserve Sacrament." Father Nestor gestured to the neatly wrapped bundle under his clothes. Seeing the blank look on his face, Father Nestor explained. "The Eucharist. We keep extra here in the tabernacle in case of an emergency, but the tabernacle is too large for me to hide."

"But why are you taking it with you?" Marko asked in confusion.

Father Nestor looked up in surprise. "You don't think we would leave the Body and Blood of Christ unguarded? If the priest here fled without it, he would have had no choice. But we do, and we will not leave it behind."

"Spare Father Nestor from having to climb back down, would you, Marko?" interrupted Father Ignatios, "and put the tabernacle back with my note next to the chalices." Marko, still confused but unwilling to ask any more questions, scampered down the rough ladder and reached up his hands for the paper and the golden box called a tabernacle. He read Father Ignatios's spiky handwriting in the sputtering lantern light. "We have taken the Chrism and Sacrament. May God be with you. Fathers Nestor, Ignatios, and Kosmas." Marko placed the note next to the chalices and carefully set the tabernacle on top to hold it in place.

Once Marko had emerged, Father Ignatios replaced the floorboards while Father Nestor wrapped the icon of Saint Phanourios in the old cassock. Marko was surprised to see the abbot's fingers cooperating, and without looking up, the monk said, "My hands don't work as well as they used to, but that doesn't mean that they don't work at all."

"Why aren't we hiding the icon down below?" Marko asked.

Father Nestor continued his work, not answering for a long time. Marko thought perhaps he hadn't heard the question and opened his mouth to ask again when Father Nestor finally said, "This one we will take with us."

"There is enough oil in the jar to fill the presence light," Father Kosmas told Father Nestor before Marko could press for more information, and the abbot nodded. Father Kosmas walked to the altar and poured a few last drops of oil into a small lamp. "This is the presence light," Father Kosmas explained. "It is always left lit on the altar because the Body and Blood are in the tabernacle."

"But aren't we taking that with us?" Marko pointed out.

Father Kosmas opened his mouth, paused for a long moment, and barked a single loud laugh.

Father Nestor smiled and motioned for him to continue. "Fill it anyway," he said, "and we will leave it in the care of the angels."

Father Ignatios found a broom and swept the floor. "Why?" asked Marko. "It's just going to get dusty again, and there's no one here to see it."

"This is the house of the Lord, Marko. Any task, any work done for the glory of God is holy," he replied. "Besides, I like to pray with my hands and feet, along with my voice. I expect I will always want to sweep any church I visit." He put the broom away and led the way out. Father Kosmas followed with the icon, and Father Ignatios pulled the door closed behind them.

Marko squinted in the bright afternoon sunlight. It had taken only an hour to rescue the icons and put the church back to rights, and the busyness had driven all other thoughts from his mind. But now they were back outside, and all his present horrors resurfaced. He quickened his pace, almost running to keep up with Father Kosmas's long strides. Father Ignatios and Father Nestor hurried behind them.

The streets were full of people. Some were heavily laden like those they had seen on the road outside the city. Others, who had decided to stay, stood in their doorways or looked out of their windows, silently watching as neighbors and friends fled. Sprinkled between his countrymen, on every street corner and in all the open shops, were soldiers.

Marko flinched away from each unfamiliar uniform, but the monks, while cautious, showed no fear. Their backs straight and their eyes forward, they strode boldly down the streets.

"Aren't you afraid?" Marko finally whispered to Father Kosmas.

"Terrified," replied the monk bluntly. "But if God is for us, who then shall be against us?" He smiled kindly at the young boy.

Father Nestor asked for directions from the bystanders, blessing each of them as they navigated the streets. They turned a corner, and Marko knew where he was. The blue domes of his home church loomed ahead, and his stomach tied itself into a knot. Home was close.

CHAPTER 13

THEY STOPPED TO CATCH their breath on the steps of Agia Irini. The monks made rapid plans in low voices, but Marko paid little attention. He was preoccupied with a nightmarish vision of his parents opening their door and being disappointed to see him. He shook his head, trying to rid himself of the image.

His guilt raged, and the world was suddenly too much to bear. The city had fallen, the enemy occupied the island, his family surely despised him, and Elias . . . oh, Elias. Even the monks would loathe him once they knew what he had done. He was catapulted backward to that fateful moment on the beach, telling Elias to stay there and play, just for a little bit.

The monks were distracted, and he wandered around the corner of the church as Father Nestor said, "The ships in the harbor are surely filling. If we want to look for a berth, we must go soon. Marko—"

Marko heard nothing else. In the tumult of the day, he had forgotten where he was, what else was at Agia Irini, and why he had refused to cross the threshold in over a year. He gasped in shock, and the sound brought the three monks hurrying to see what was amiss. Father Kosmas careened into him, and they fell in a heap on the grass. In front of them were long rows of wooden crosses.

"No," he whispered, his voice hoarse and broken. Marko clenched his eyes shut so he wouldn't have to see. How, in all of the places in all of the world, had he ended up here? He sat on the ground. No one made a sound. Marko felt a cassock brush his face and knew one of the other monks was near, but he would not open his eyes to see who it was. He didn't care.

Marko could not remain here forever. Sooner or later, the monks would ask questions, or an enemy battalion would march down the street. His eyes flew open, dark and flashing. He was angry at the ships and the armies who had attacked them, at the constant starvation and all of the pain he had suffered in the last year. He was furious with his family, but most of all his brother, and even

God Himself. Marko stood abruptly and stormed away. His flight lasted three strides, then the fight drained from him. His legs gave way, and he dropped on the ground in front of the smallest whitewashed cross in the graveyard.

Marko sat in a heap. The three monks stationed themselves around him. He reached out a limp hand toward the cross but stopped a hairsbreadth away, unable and unwilling to confirm where he already knew he was.

"Marko," said Father Ignatios quietly, his voice gentle. "Who is Elias?"

The name was a knife to his soul, and Marko bent double, his arms wrapped his body. Slowly, so slowly, he looked up. Crosses stretched to his right and behind him—in neat rows, marking the graves of neighbors and friends, distant relations and acquaintances, but he saw none of them. He had eyes only for the one in front of him, the cross that marked the final resting place of his baby brother.

Marko spoke haltingly, painfully laying bare the details of his shame; how his mother had sent him to take Elias on an outing so she could rest, and how he had fought and complained, wanting to explore caves and fish with his friends, not play nanny to the toddler who followed him everywhere. He had told Elias to stay put while he swam, but Elias had not listened, insisting on imitating everything his older brother did, and followed him into the surf. Marko's voice broke, and his body shook as he relived the horror. How the undertow had pulled the small boy down into the waves, and how he heard that final cry for help, Elias screaming his name as Marko swam as fast as his arms would allow, his frantic strokes slicing the water and the salty spray splashing his face.

"I wasn't fast enough. I was too late," Marko whispered, his voice breaking as his shaking hand touched the cross. "I got him out of the water, but he wasn't breathing, and I couldn't . . ." Father Ignatios lowered himself next to Marko and reached for him, and this time Marko went willingly, leaning back into the monk's strong arms. For the first time, finally, he cried for his brother. Marko sobbed until he thought he would break, screaming his anger and grief and brokenness into the cassock-clad shoulder. When his throat was sore, he took a shuddering breath and turned away to hook his arms around his brother's cross, and Marko wept into the dust of Elias's grave.

When the storm had passed and Marko had no tears left, Father Ignatios laid his hand on his shoulder. Marko allowed the monk to help him up and leaned against him as they left the graveyard.

"Show us the way home, Marko," Father Nestor said. Marko picked up his leaden feet and turned back onto the street. The afternoon was waning. If there was any dinner to be had, it would be almost time to eat. Marko thought of the table where he had shared so many meals with his family, and he swallowed a hiccup. "I don't know what to do," he confessed quietly.

"About what?" Father Nestor asked softly. He walked on Marko's other side, close enough that Marko was able to barely make out the smell of incense that permeated his clothing.

"My parents," Marko sighed, his breath shaking as it whooshed out of him. "They hate me."

"No." Father Nestor shook his head, and his tangled

salt-and-pepper hair rustled behind him. "They are grieving, with you and for you. What happened was a horrible accident."

"It feels like my fault," Marko admitted, emotion rising in his throat and making it difficult to breathe.

Father Nestor was silent for a moment. "Marko," he said finally, "tell me about your parents."

Marko was startled. "What do you mean?"

"How do you get along with them?"

Marko slumped against Father Ignatios. The younger monk tightened his hand on Marko's shoulder and propelled him forward. Marko pointed, and they turned down a narrow alleyway. "My papa..." he said, the words thick on his tongue and hard to find. "My papa is very tall. He looks more like Irene, my sister. I look mostly like my mama," he said, glancing at Father Nestor. The abbot nodded.

"We used to play together, me and Papa and Elias. Throwing a ball, or just...just laughing. We milked the goats together, and Papa would move the pails, and we would try and aim the milk, like a contest. But after

Elias died . . ." He paused. "Papa doesn't laugh anymore."

"He stopped hugging me," Marko added after a long moment. "It was like I had a sickness, some kind of disease that made bad things happen around me."

Father Ignatios made an inarticulate sound in his throat, but Marko plowed on. "It started to hurt when Mama tried to give me a hug or kiss me goodnight. So I made her stop. But that didn't help either."

"Grief does strange things to people." Father Nestor sighed. "It makes them forget parts of who they are."

"Mama said that she wished she hadn't sent Elias out with me, that she thought he would be safe, but he wasn't," Marko blurted in a rush of pain. "I never knew that, until she said it."

"She said that to you?"

Marko shook his head. "To Papa."

Father Nestor nodded. "What else?"

Marko was confused. He could see that night in his mind; he could feel the emotion keenly, but the memory itself was blurry. "Nothing, I think. She saw me, but I left."

"And?"

Marko forced his thoughts back. "And that night, I slept with the goats. I woke up and she had covered me up with a blanket."

Father Kosmas smiled. "That sounds like a motherly thing to do."

"Marko, I'm confused," Father Nestor said, shaking his black and silver head. "When did your parents tell you that they no longer loved you?"

Marko was flabbergasted. "They . . . they didn't."

"Then when did they tell you that they wanted you to go away, or that they didn't want you to be their son anymore?"

Marko began to wilt. His head sunk down to his chest until his ears were nearly level with his shoulders and his knees felt weak. "They didn't," he whispered.

Father Nestor pondered this for a long moment. "Then why do you fear reuniting with your family so much?"

Marko gestured helplessly. "Because my brother is dead, and it is my fault. How could they not hate me?"

"Ah," Father Nestor sighed. "Yes." He stared long at

Marko until Marko lifted his eyes and met the monk's gaze. "I am certain that your parents do not hate you, Marko. They are grieving."

"I am also certain," he continued, "that they forgive you. It is always harder for us to forgive ourselves, to let go of our guilt and shame, especially when we wish we could go back and make different decisions and choices. God has a plan for all of us." Marko opened his mouth to argue, but the abbot lifted a hand to stop him. "Even our poor choices can be made new by the grace of God."

Grief stole Marko's voice. He groaned softly and pressed further into the comfort of Father Ignatios, inhaling great, shuddering breaths. He was painfully, acutely aware of the gaping emptiness in his heart that was the exact shape and size of his small brother.

The alleyway ended and spilled them onto Marko's street. His steps faltered. The monks surrounded him as he paused, and Father Ignatios tightened his arm around Marko. "Do you remember when I told you about my friend Stavros?"

Marko nodded.

"For a long time, the only way to relieve my guilt was to punish myself in every way I could think of. But punishment was not the answer. I had to forgive myself. Once you learn to do this, you can begin to heal."

"How?" Marko whispered.

"It takes time. Time and God." Father Ignatios sighed. "And in your case, I think also reconciling with your parents."

Marko slowly shook his head, misery overwhelming him.

"Have courage, Marko," Father Kosmas said. He stood in front of Marko, the third side of a triangle of support, and his towering bulk blocked the late afternoon sun. Marko was able to look up without squinting, and the sun shone around the monk's ebony head like a halo. "Remember what God told the Prophet Isaiah: 'Fear not, for I am with you. Do not go astray, for I am your God who strengthens you; and I will help and secure you with My righteous right hand.'"

Marko sighed heavily. "What do we do now?"

"We take you home," Father Nestor said gently. "And we will see what God has in store."

Marko swallowed hard. "What if they're not home? What if they left without me?"

"Let's find out, Marko. Lead the way, and we will follow."

Marko could endure the suspense no longer. He raced the short distance to his front door, so fast that only Father Kosmas was able to keep up. A tangled knot of emotions warred inside him. He was terrified that his parents would be home, but equally afraid that they would not.

The doors and windows of his house had been locked and barred against intruders, but Marko had snuck in and out dozens of times and wasted no time climbing up the backyard pomegranate tree and through the window into his bedroom. He ran through the small house, opening every door and shouting for his parents and Irene.

The house was empty.

By the time he reached the kitchen, his steps had slowed to a dull plod and his arms felt like stone. He lifted the bar on the back door to let the monks in and dropped into a seat at the deserted kitchen table. "They're gone."

Father Ignatios sat quietly with him, saying nothing

as Father Kosmas searched each room again and Father Nestor went to inquire with the neighbors. Father Kosmas returned empty-handed, but Father Nestor had news.

"They were forced to evacuate," he reported grimly. "Suleiman put Commander de L'Isle, his aides, and their families on the first ship, and it set sail two days ago, before the ink on the treaty was even dry." He sat at the table and waited until Marko's eyes met his own. "Marko, your neighbor told me that your mother refused to leave without you, that the soldiers had to force her on the boat, and that she was hoarse from searching for you. She did not go willingly."

Marko leaned his head on his arms. Through the fog in his brain, he dimly registered that someone was saying his name. Looking up, he saw Father Nestor waiting for him to acknowledge his question. Marko furrowed his brow, and Father Nestor repeated, "Do you have any family that does not live on Rhodes?"

Marko nodded. "I have an aunt in Ierissos. Papa said if he and Mama were separated, that was where they should go."

The monks looked at each other with a combination of amazement and surprise. Father Nestor glanced heavenward and barked a short laugh. "Well, there is our answer." He turned to Marko and said, "Our plan has been to reunite you with your parents, then see what God laid out for us after we had done that. Ierissos is the closest town to Athos, the Holy Mountain."

Marko was confused but distracted by Father Ignatios, who was laughing in delighted relief. "Athos is the home of all monks. We did not know what God planned for our future when we left for Panagia Filerimos. But we have said over and over to each other, if no other destination presents itself, we will simply go to Athos. God be praised!"

"You will come with us, and we will deliver you to your aunt," Father Nestor said. "God willing, we will be able to get word through her to your parents, and you will be reunited."

Marko looked up at him, unnamed emotion flickering dimly in his chest. "You . . . you will take me all the way to Ierissos?" he said dumbly. "But it's so far!"

"Psshh." Father Kosmas blew air from his lips. He looked sternly at Marko. "You think we would abandon you?" Marko looked hopefully at the monk, who frowned then crossed his eyes. Marko smiled halfheartedly, and Father Kosmas winked.

He wiped his face on his sleeve, wrinkling his nose at the smell that had accumulated over the past few days of rough living. Father Ignatios noticed his distaste and motioned him toward the door. "Go wash up and pack a bag. We will leave when you are ready."

Marko climbed the stairs to his room. He changed out of his filthy clothes and gathered spares from a peg behind his door, noticing that some of his favorite things were gone. He stuffed breeches and two shirts into the depths of an old haversack he found under his parents' bed, along with his carving knife and the collection of small wooden animals that Papa had made for him over the years that he had hidden under his bed. Marko wondered what else he should take.

He returned to his parents' room and opened the drawer of Mama's bedside table. They must have had enough time to quickly pack before retreating, for her dresses were gone, but one of her scarves had been left behind. Marko picked it up off the floor and brought it to his face. It still smelled like his mother, her own scent mingled with the beeswax and chamomile of the salve she had mixed. The clean, sunshine scent caused his heart to lurch.

He stopped back in his room and reached inside his dirty shirt for the dried and slightly crumpled piece of parchment hidden there. He wrapped the missive for his father in his mother's scarf and hid the small package in the depths of his pack.

Father Nestor had rummaged through the cupboards and was stirring something over a small fire. Marko leaned over and sniffed, wrinkling his nose at the odd combination of herbs. "There wasn't much food left," Father Nestor said by way of explanation. "But we have to try and eat something before we go." Marko nodded but was utterly unenthused at the thought of drinking the strange broth. He ducked his head into the root cellar, but it was empty. Sudden inspiration grabbed him, and he ran to the backyard.

Their flock of chickens had been severely depleted, but he knew their habits. It did not take him long to flush the last remnant of Irene's favorite pets out of hiding. The chicken was scrawny, bedraggled, and utterly disinclined to be caught, but Marko was hungry. He chased the bird through the overgrown grass of the yard before making a flying leap to tackle the hen. He held her tightly, the chicken squawking in outrage, and walked to the chopping block. "I'm sorry, Irene," Marko muttered.

He had never butchered a chicken alone but had worked alongside his parents enough times to know the steps. Twenty minutes later, he appeared in the kitchen door, framed by the setting sun, and proudly handed a flabbergasted Father Nestor the plucked and roughly gutted bird. Father Ignatios laughed out loud and quickly cut the chicken into pieces with a sharp knife that had been left behind. The bird stewed quickly, seasoned further by the tiny bit of salt Marko found stashed in the cellar.

Marko toured the backyard while the chicken cooked. His future was uncertain, but there was comfort here in the familiar confines of his home. A single feather lay at the base of the pomegranate tree, and he recognized the tail feather of their rooster. It was bright, multicolored, and perfect. He tucked it into the knot of Mama's scarf for Irene.

Father Ignatios uncovered the icon of the mysterious Saint Phanourios and set it on the table to watch over them while they ate. The chicken was stringy and tough, flavored with Father Nestor's haphazard assortment of herbs, and it left a strange aftertaste in the back of his mouth. Marko thought it was the best thing he had ever eaten. They ate quickly, finishing the last of the broth as soon as it was cool enough to swallow. Marko still wasn't full, but the chicken had been a gift. He had searched the rest of the house while the soup boiled, but there was nothing else to be found. Even the goats were gone, dead or stolen—Marko had no idea—and he swallowed his heartache, feeling briefly foolish for mourning the loss.

"Maybe there will be food on the boats," he said to the monks.

Father Kosmas snorted and shook his curly head.

"I may die of amazement if there is," he said under his breath.

"Father Kosmas, have faith," Father Nestor reprimanded quietly. "Has not God provided for us thus far? And now we are able to leave, with the Holy Chrism, the Eucharist, this icon, and our friend Marko here."

Father Kosmas crossed himself. "You are right. Forgive me."

Father Nestor gathered Marko and the monks together. "Lord," he prayed, "we ask for your blessing upon our journey, and we hold fast to the words of the prophet Jeremiah: 'For I know the plans I have for you, says the LORD; plans for good, and not for evil, to give you a future and a hope.' Keep us safe as we travel, deliver us in peace to the Holy Mountain, and reunite Marko with his family. In the name of the Father and of the Son and of the Holy Spirit." The monks crossed themselves and Marko imitated without thinking, his hand tracing the familiar pattern over his forehead and shoulders.

"To the boats," Father Kosmas said grimly.

CHAPTER 14

MARKO COLLAPSED on the deck, his body clumsy with exhaustion. He wedged his torso into a corner between two large wooden barrels and wrapped his arms around his bent legs. They were on a ship. He could hardly believe it.

The docks were crowded, every last person starving and desperate. They had spent the evening and early morning hours waiting with everyone else for their turn to board. The monks were reluctant to sleep, fearing that they would miss the call. They passed the time silently working the knots on their prayer ropes. Marko dozed fitfully, leaning on Father Ignatios and waking when the long line inched forward. He had eaten nothing since the chicken soup, and his gnawing hunger prevented any real sleep, although a woman he had vaguely recognized as the mother of one of Irene's friends spotted him in line and quietly pressed a sliver of dried meat in his hand. Marko tried to share the small morsel with the monks, but they refused. He inhaled the food, feeling mingled shame and guilt, but he was so famished that he almost didn't care.

They had stumbled up the gangplank in the inky blackness. The darkness was broken only by lanterns hanging from large hooks in the masts and dangling from the rigging. A sailor grunted and pointed in the direction of the bow. Marko rested his head on his knees, thankful to finally be sitting. The monks dropped themselves to the deck next to him, contorting their bodies closer together as more and more people packed onto the ship. The soldiers had orders to board everyone who would fit, and they loaded the ship until it sat so low in the water that Marko feared they would sink.

Father Nestor sat closest to Marko, the icon of Saint Phanourios nestled behind the monk for safekeeping. He rearranged their meager belongings to create enough space for Marko to lie down. "Sleep, Marko," he said. "We are safe enough here."

Marko did not wait to be told again.

When he woke, a faint nausea replaced the pangs of

hunger. Marko had made no attempt during the night to make sense of his surroundings. Now, the sun was high in the sky, and Marko blinked painfully as his eyes adjusted to the onslaught of light.

They were in the front of the ship. As they crested each wave and came down, sea spray tossed up and over them. Father Ignatios and Father Kosmas were sleeping sitting up. Father Kosmas's head was tilted backward, his mouth gaping open as rasping snores erupted from his deep chest. Father Ignatios still held his prayer rope loosely in his hand.

Only Father Nestor was awake. The icon of Saint Phanourios lay unwrapped in his lap. He had draped the dilapidated cassock over his head and arms, forming an open-sided tent to protect the icon from sea spray. He smiled out of the opening as Marko sat up and stretched. "How are you feeling?" he asked quietly.

Marko made a face, one hand absentmindedly rubbing his stomach. "Not well," he admitted.

Father Nestor grimaced in sympathy. "Take heart. The boats are dropping us off at the nearest Greek port, which is Crete. We will be there by this evening. God willing, there will be food as well as dry land."

Marko's stomach jumped at the thought of food then collapsed instantly back in on itself with a roll of nausea. "Can we not talk about food? I don't know if I'm hungry or sick right now."

Father Nestor smiled and nodded his graying head. "Of course. Come and look instead at this icon. When we found it, we did not have time to really study it before leaving. I have been thinking that surely, some part of it would remind me of the saint's story, but I have not been successful."

"Do we know anything?" Marko asked, scooting closer and ducking under the protection of the umbrella of fabric next to Father Nestor.

"Only what I can learn from the icon itself. If we look here," Father Nestor pointed with a twisted finger, "we see the saint standing with his sword and armor in the center. A cloak like the one he is wearing is usually used in iconography to depict a soldier, so I think we can assume that is, in fact, what he was."

Marko pointed to the smaller scenes around the perimeter of the icon. "Then what about these?"

"Those, I believe, are all the tortures the saint endured. We see him here, questioned by a magistrate—possibly Roman—and defending his faith. But in the next he is being beaten on the head and mouth with rocks. Yet he remains patient. And we see in another part that he is now on the ground, being beaten again with sticks and clubs."

Marko shivered as he watched Father Nestor point out each of the illustrations in turn. The saint, now naked as soldiers rip his flesh with iron weapons, and then praying in prison. Phanourios before the magistrates, his face calm as he defends his faith, then punished for his defense by having his body scorched by fire.

"What is that?" Marko asked in horror, as Father Nestor's finger hovered over a particularly bloody scene.

"Some kind of mechanical torture device," Father Nestor said. "He is tied to it, and it looks like as they rotate the bars, his bones will be crushed."

"That's awful," Marko said vehemently.

"The martyrs endured great and terrible things for

Christ, Marko. Look at his face, though. Even though he suffers so greatly, his face is peaceful and patient. Here in the next panel, it looks as though he was thrown to wild beasts, but they refused to harm him. They are lying about him like lambs around a shepherd."

Marko pointed to the next illustration. "Is he being crushed under a boulder?"

Father Nestor nodded. "And here, the next one, he has hot coals on his hands as they are trying to force him to make pagan sacrifices. Look! Do you see the dragon? Icons will use dragons to represent the demons. The dragon is flying away and crying, because he is defeated. Saint Phanourios had remarkable courage, Marko. Here in the last scene—this must be his martyrdom. He was burned alive in a kiln. But even then, at the moment of his death, we see that he is praying."

Marko furrowed his brow. "I don't think I would be praying if I was being burned alive."

Father Nestor smiled, the crinkles in the corners of his eyes matching the wrinkles on his forehead. "You would be surprised, Marko." He touched the icon reverently.

"God grants us strength, and peace, and joy, even in the hardest circumstances."

A familiar pain flamed in his chest, constricting his heart with an invisible fist. Marko swallowed and looked out of the tent opening into the boundless sky. "I am afraid," he admitted to Father Nestor.

"I know, Marko," he replied gently. "You are enduring your own great trial right now. But God knows this and has not forgotten you."

"I miss my mother," Marko said quietly. "She should hate me for what I did, but I want her anyway."

Father Nestor leaned his shoulder against Marko's. "Your mother does not hate you, Marko. She loves you because you are hers, like your sister and your brother. Death does not change this; neither does distance."

"How do you know?" Marko leaned his head back against the barrel behind him.

"Many years ago, I had a child," Father Nestor said quietly. "She lived only a day, and my wife breathed her last that same hour. And yet I love her because she is mine."

Marko bottled his shock unsuccessfully, and Father Nestor chuckled softly. "I was a married priest before I was a monk. Widowed priests do not remarry, and so I chose to enter the monastery."

"What was your baby's name?" Marko whispered.

Father Nestor pulled the cassock off of their heads and wrapped the icon gently in the black fabric before he answered, a small catch in his voice. "Maria. I pray for her every day, and now I will add Elias to that prayer."

Marko sighed. "I'm not sure that I believe in God."

Father Nestor did not seem shocked. "Why do you think that is?"

Marko leaned back, looking up into the sky. The water crashed against the boat's hull, and a lone gull whirled and cried mournfully above the mast. Marko pointed it out to Father Nestor, avoiding the question. "It's strange that the bird is so far out to sea and all by itself."

"Perhaps it was resting on the ship, or a stray wind blew it out this far."

Marko exhaled in an annoyed huff. "So, it's lost. Everything around here is lost. I'm lost, the bird is lost, even this Saint Phanourios is lost." Sudden anger welled up inside of him, and he whirled on Father Nestor. "You want to know why I don't believe in God? My brother is dead. He was just a baby. What kind of God does that?" Marko looked around in frustration, desperately wanting something to break, to destroy. Finding nothing at hand, he drove his fist into the nearest barrel. Gasping at the pain, Marko fought back tears, instead resting his head on his knees, his wounded hand hanging limply at his side.

Father Nestor sat quietly until Marko's breathing regulated, then he reached carefully to inspect his bruises. "Marko," he said quietly, "God does not desire death. He created man as a perfect being with free will, and man fell. We say during the liturgy: 'Through man, sin came into the world, and through sin, death.' God did not take your brother."

"Then who did?" Marko pulled his hand away.

"Sin," Father Nestor replied firmly. "Sin and a fallen world. God is love, Marko. Love, not death."

Marko pressed his face harder into his knees as Father Nestor continued. "There is beauty of life and love in

Christ, Marko." He tapped the icon in his hands, reinforcing his words with thump after thump. "The pain you feel at your brother's death? God the Father knows that pain. His son died, too."

Marko squirmed in place, but Father Nestor was not deterred. "The loneliness you feel? Jesus knows that loneliness. He was abandoned by His closest friends as He hung on the Cross. He knows your grief, and He knows your agony. And, Marko, He suffers with you."

"Then, why?" Marko cried out, lifting his grieving face to meet Father Nestor's eyes. "Why did He let Elias die?" A spray of ocean water misted his face.

Father Nestor handed him a handkerchief from his cassock pocket. "We cannot know the mind of God, Marko. But I will tell you what I do know: Christ is risen. He is risen from the dead, trampling down death by death, and upon those in the tombs, bestowing life."

Father Nestor placed his arm around Marko and pulled the young boy close. "You have much grief and pain, Marko. God will comfort you, but you have to let Him," he said quietly.

"How?" Marko choked.

"All you have to do is ask."

"I don't think I can," Marko whispered.

"Let me help you," Father Nestor said gently, and he bowed his head as Marko's shoulders shuddered under his arm. Father Nestor prayed for consolation and for peace and then sat quietly whispering the Jesus Prayer.

When his storm had passed, Marko lifted his head and saw the gull perched on a barrel nearby, its beady eye watching him curiously. "Do you think he will find his way home?"

Father Nestor watched the bird preen his feathers. "Yes. So will this icon, and so will you."

Marko felt a body stirring close by and scrubbed at his face. Father Ignatios sat up and stretched unconvincingly. Marko knew that everyone had likely heard his conversation with Father Nestor, or at the very least, had been awakened by his one-sided punching match with the barrel. But he was too exhausted to be embarrassed.

"How long until we reach land?" Father Ignatios asked.

Father Nestor shook off the cassock covering, shaded his eyes, and looked up at the sun. "Not long. It is about twelve hours from Rhodes to Crete, and we have been on board for close to that. Once we land, we will look for a monastery, and God willing, there will be food."

"Yes, please." Marko clutched his stomach.

"Perhaps someone on Crete will have heard of our Saint Phanourios," added Father Ignatios.

A shout rang out from high above them in the crow's nest. Marko didn't understand the language, but the instant change in demeanor of the people crowded on deck told him that land had been sighted. Several people nearby stood, looking over the bow to see the land for themselves. Marko joined them, stretching his arms high over his head. He rose on the tips of his toes and leaned back, feeling his back pop in several places up his spine.

"Ohh," he groaned, shaking out his arms and bouncing a little on his feet. It felt good to stretch, but the movement jostled his already cranky stomach. He watched Father Nestor carefully bundle Saint Phanourios back into his wrappings, and his mind recalled the many scenes of torture the icon depicted. Cautiously, he reached out his heart and attempted a prayer for the first time since he had held Elias's limp body in his arms. "Saint Phanourios, if you're there, please help me find my family."

CHAPTER 15

THE MARINA IN CRETE was overflowing with refugees. Marko struggled not to be lost in the crowd as they fought their way through the press of people. "Where are we going?" Marko had to shout in order to be heard over the noise.

"Anywhere but here!" Father Kosmas shouted back. His body towered over nearly everyone, and he squared his wide shoulders to plow a furrow through the chaos. Most people took one look at his bulk and moved to make space; following him was like following Moses when he parted the Red Sea.

"We need to find a church," Father Ignatios said when the crowds thinned and they could hear each other again.

Marko pointed at a woman walking toward them with a basket over her arm. "Should we ask her?" Without waiting for an answer, he walked up to the woman.

Hunger must be making me brave, he thought, before asking the woman, as politely as he could, "Could you please tell me where a church is?"

The startled woman pointed down a nearby street. "Agios Minas is that way. But all the churches are full of refugees from the boats."

Marko's shoulders sagged in disappointment.

"Are you just off the boats too?" she asked kindly.

Marko nodded.

"When was the last time you ate?"

Marko shrugged. "Yesterday."

The woman clicked her tongue in reproach and grumbled something inaudible under her breath. She dug into her cloth-covered basket and handed Marko a loaf of thick, crusty bread. Without thinking, he gnawed an end off of the loaf before she could change her mind. In sadness she watched him chew. Marko thanked her and gestured to the three monks waiting for him. "My friends haven't eaten either," he said hopefully.

The woman's eyes widened. She crossed the cobbled street with Marko and handed the rest of the contents of her basket to the monks. Marko was astonished as another loaf of bread, several polished red apples, and a round block of creamy goat's cheese appeared. They received the simple food with gratitude, pulling apart the soft cheese and smearing it on rough chunks of bread. Marko bit into an apple and closed his eyes in bliss as the sweet juices exploded on his tongue. He made a low sound of utter enjoyment, and the woman smiled.

"If I were you," she said hesitantly, "I would skip Agios Minas and go to the Toplou Monastery to the north. The church here is overrun, and the monks might have more to offer."

At the sound of the word *monastery*, the monks lifted their heads in unison. "How far?" asked Father Ignatios, his green eyes brightening.

The woman shrugged. "A day's walk, maybe."

"Can you do it, Marko?" asked Father Nestor.

Marko nodded. "I can even take a turn carrying the icon," he offered.

Father Ignatios smiled and handed the icon to Marko,

who stowed his remaining bread in a pocket and carefully wiped his fingers on his pants before accepting the wrapped bundle. He saw the woman eyeing it curiously, so he pulled back the tattered covering. She stretched out a hand and gently touched the silver of the saint's tunic. "Have you ever heard of Saint Phanourios?" Father Nestor asked.

She shook her head and looked at them expectantly, clearly thinking they were going to tell her about him. Father Ignatios smiled faintly and told her a brief version of their strange finding of the mysterious saint. Her eyes grew wide, then wider as she glanced from Marko to the icon he held. "Perhaps the monks at Toplou will know of him," she said as she adjusted the empty basket on her arm. Father Nestor blessed her, and she kissed his hand before returning to her path down the street.

Their boat had landed in the late afternoon, and the sun was low in the sky as Marko and the monks navigated their way out of the city. They slept on the side of the road under the boughs of several fruit trees, soft grasses pillowing their exhausted bodies. Marko was the first awake, and he chewed slowly on the small piece of bread he had saved in his pocket. He was momentarily surprised to see pomegranates hanging ripe on the branches above him and had to remind himself that not every island in the Mediterranean had been stripped bare. He reached up and picked the largest one.

He rolled onto his belly and propped himself up on his elbows. Using his mother's knife, he cut several deep slits in the ruby peel and broke it open, revealing the jeweled arils inside. Juice dripped down his fingers as he dug at the center of the fruit, popping a handful of tiny red orbs into his mouth. "I love food," he murmured happily, and his eyes closed in delight as the fresh taste exploded on his tongue.

Father Kosmas slept next to Marko, sprawled out and snoring. The leather strap had loosened from his hair, and his unruly black curls flew in every direction. Marko thought that he, Irene, and Mama could all have fit in the hollow of grass that Father Kosmas had nestled into.

Before the monk had fallen asleep, he had stretched out on his back and carefully placed the straight-sided black cap that he wore over his face. Marko raised his eyebrows at this, and Father Kosmas said, "To keep the spiders from nesting in my mouth." His wide black eyes had stared innocently at Marko then snapped shut, and he was asleep in less than a minute. Marko was still unsure if the monk had been serious or not.

The sun was not quite over the horizon, but the dusky gray of early morning gave enough light for Marko to see a small black spider hanging from the end of its silk thread over Father Kosmas. The skoufos had fallen from his face, and the spider drifted over the monk's mouth, blowing to and fro like a pendulum as Father Kosmas exhaled. Marko rolled on his belly and reached up, gently pinching the silk string and lowering the spider into the grass by his feet. It scuttled away to safety, and he carefully replaced the cap over Father Kosmas's mouth. The monk twitched in his sleep but kept snoring.

The icon was nestled carefully between Marko and Father Ignatios, who was curled tightly in a ball on Marko's other side. The monks had asked everyone they had met on the boat if they had heard of Saint Phanourios, but no one had. Marko wiped his hands on the side of his trousers and gently lifted the icon without disturbing the monks, holding it in his lap until they woke.

Marko carried Saint Phanourios as they walked that morning. A corner of the cassock wrapping flapped in the soft breeze, revealing the saint's face, and Marko felt a strange kinship with the mysterious martyr. *We're both lost*, he thought to himself while he marveled at the scenery around them. Crete felt like paradise after the desolation of Rhodes. Farmers waved as they passed, and more than one kind woman, taking pity on their haggard appearance, handed them fruit and cheese from her market basket. One farmer's wife even had cookies. She was Marko's favorite.

I don't know where my family is, and you don't have a church anymore. Marko's internal communication with the saint continued. A long-eared gray rabbit startled him from his one-sided conversation as it leapt unexpectedly out of the wild grass on the side of the road. Marko whooped in surprise, stumbling backward into Father Kosmas. Marko laughed a little as he caught his breath, but the encounter had knocked more of the cassock covering the icon away, revealing several of the gruesome scenes of the saint's torture. *You were brave*, he told the saint, sighing in frustration. *I'm just frightened.*

The sky was filled with birdsong. He folded the dilapidated cassock back over the icon and turned to Father Ignatios, who was walking beside him. "Father Nestor says that God grants peace and strength and joy to people, even in the midst of trials."

Father Ignatios looked momentarily startled, but nodded.

"Do you think . . ." Marko drew in a deep breath. "Do you think God grants courage as well?"

"Of course he does," the monk answered. "We have only to ask."

A soft breeze from the coast sprung up and cooled them as they walked. Marko turned so the wind fell more fully on his face. He was wonderfully, gloriously full. The struggles and problems they had faced and would continue to face seemed a little more surmountable with a belly full of food. A sudden movement caught his eye, and he turned to see that the breeze he was enjoying was pestering his companions, tossing the monks' long beards into their faces.

"They're a hazard sometimes," Father Ignatios said ruefully as he tucked the ends of his chestnut beard into the front of his cassock. "I got mine tangled in the fishing nets once while I was hauling them in." He touched the lump on his long nose. "That's how I broke my nose. When I tried to yank my beard out of the net, a weight from the side smashed into my face."

Marko grimaced.

"Mine is always full of sawdust," Father Kosmas chimed in. He looked down and spotted a piece of fig that was caught in the black tangle. "Or food," he added, cheerfully popping the morsel in his mouth.

Marko yawned. The breeze had been brief, and now the high, hot sun beat mercilessly, and a constant trickle of sweat ran down the back of his neck. All he wanted was to sleep in a bed again. He was quiet as they walked, too tired to do much more than continue to put one foot in front of another.

Father Kosmas defied exhaustion, swinging his strong arms back and forth robustly and twisting his head to look in all directions while he hummed. Marko vaguely recognized the tune. They rounded a gentle corner in the path, and Father Kosmas switched from humming to singing. He possessed a powerful voice, a clear bass that bellowed from his gigantic lungs. He startled a nearby bird from its perch as he launched into the *evlogitaria*. "Blessed are You, O Lord, teach me Your statutes."

Father Nestor smiled. Apparently used to Father Kosmas bursting into song, he joined in with his own soft tenor, and the two monks chanted the hymn. Marko looked to Father Ignatios, expecting him to sing as well, but the monk was silent, his face peaceful and soft as he listened to the voices of his companions.

When the hymn ended, Father Kosmas returned to humming and loped to the side of the road to inspect something that had caught his eye. Marko looked at Father Ignatios. "Why didn't you sing?" he asked curiously.

"Why didn't you?" the monk replied in a light voice.

Marko was taken aback. "I don't know all the words,"

he said, narrowing his eyes. "But you're a monk," he bravely teased. "What's your excuse?"

Father Ignatios chuckled. "I can't carry a tune," he said. "I prefer to just listen."

"You can't carry a tune?" Marko repeated in astonishment. He had never met a monk who couldn't sing. Father Kosmas popped up beside him. "Not even if he had a bucket," he informed Marko seriously, and Marko laughed. The sound startled him. How long had it been since he had laughed?

The monks smiled as one at Marko's laughter but said nothing. The four of them walked down the road in easy companionship, rejuvenated by song and enjoying the beauty of the day.

Father Kosmas took the icon from Marko so he could rest his arms, but his thoughts continually returned to the saint. No one knew where Saint Phanourios had come from, and Marko was keenly aware that no one really knew where he himself was heading. If his Aunt Diana even knew where to find his parents, his journey would not stop with her. The monks had Athos and their brotherhood there, and he envied their sense of belong-ing. He looked sideways at the bundle in Father Kosmas's arms. Perhaps, he thought, he and Saint Phanourios could belong to each other. *O God*, he groaned, not even realiz-ing that he was praying, *if I ever do find my family, please let my parents forgive me.*

Marko was so preoccupied with the effort of walking that he didn't notice the monastery walls until they loomed directly in front of him. Father Kosmas banged his gigan-tic fist on the wooden doors, and the four weary travelers were immediately admitted. The monks greeted them with kindness and showed Marko to a small chamber. "Clean sheets," Marko mumbled in exhausted amazement as he entered.

Father Ignatios pointed to the ewer of water and a pile of linens left on a side table. "Let us keep them that way. Here, wash before bed." Marko nodded gratefully, rins-ing days of accumulated grime off his body and sighing in pleasure at the feel of the warm water and soft towel. He changed into a nightshirt that was thoughtfully included and was just climbing into bed when he heard a soft knock.

"All is well?" Father Ignatios asked as he peeked his head around the door.

Marko nodded. "Are you going to bed, too?"

The monk nodded. "I am in the room next door with Father Nestor and Father Kosmas. We will not be far." He smiled gently at Marko and began to leave.

"Please," Marko asked sleepily, "may I keep the icon with me?"

Father Ignatios consented with a weary smile and disappeared to retrieve it from his room. He set the icon gently on a table next to the bed, and Marko was asleep before the monk closed the door, Saint Phanourios quietly keeping watch at his side.

CHAPTER 16

MARKO AND THE MONKS stayed at the monastery for a week, resting and recuperating. The long months of hunger and the last week of near starvation had severely weakened Marko. He slept for the first few days, waking only to eat some simple broth and bread before succumbing again to his pillow. Each time he fell asleep, he did so with his eyes on Saint Phanourios.

Early on the morning of the fifth day, Marko woke to the sound of the *talanton* beating a rhythmic pattern to call the monks to orthros. He surprised himself by deciding to follow them.

The paths were paved with clean, cream-colored sand and bordered by tall, spindly pine trees. The imposing stone buildings were built with towers and curved arches, complete with covered walkways that offered shade and respite from the sun. Great bushes, taller than Marko and bursting with pink and fuchsia blossoms, grew next to the rock walls and entrances.

Marko hesitated at the entrance of the church. His nose twitched. The scent of flowers gave way to the smoky incense—the smell familiar and comforting. He slid his foot along the polished marble floor, and having taken that first step, found each one after to be a little easier.

It was almost impossible to distinguish the cassock-clad men from each other, except for Father Kosmas, who stood head and shoulders above his brethren. He snuck past the billowing black sleeves and stood quietly beside him. The monk's familiar deep voice blended seamlessly with the choir, and he winked at Marko as the chanter began the evlogitaria. Marko smiled back and turned to search the faces surrounding him. He located Father Ignatios and smiled to see him standing peacefully, his eyes lifted in prayer.

Marko followed the monks to breakfast after church. It was a quiet meal; they ate without talking and listened to one of the fathers read from the Psalter. Marko was fine with that. His appetite had returned as his strength increased, and less talking meant more eating. He filled himself with hot grain porridge that was swimming in butter, cream, and honey. When his spoon scraped the bottom of his bowl, another bowl miraculously appeared at his elbow. He looked up in time to catch Father Kosmas's wink before diving in.

When the meal was finished, the abbot, Father Thomas, rang a small bell, and the monks dispersed quietly to their daily tasks. Father Ignatios whispered a request to Marko, who hurried back to his room as quickly as his bursting stomach would allow and retrieved the icon. Father Nestor had not wanted Marko disturbed while he rested, so Father Thomas had not yet seen Saint Phanourios.

Father Thomas held the icon in his hands and looked it over for a long time before reverently venerating the saint. "I've not heard of Saint Phanourios," he said, "but he was clearly a great warrior of God."

"Are we sure he is a saint, then?" asked Father Kosmas.

Marko looked at him in surprise.

"Well, no one has ever heard of him," Father Kosmas pointed out.

"We have an icon," Father Thomas said firmly. "Someone had sufficient knowledge to commission the icon, and whether that person was an iconographer or God Himself, it is enough."

Father Ignatios took the icon from the abbot and motioned Marko forward. "Father Thomas, this is Marko. His family was evacuated from Rhodes while he was trapped outside the city walls."

Father Thomas reached out a hand to bless Marko and asked him the names of his parents.

"Iakovos and Eleni. And my sister is Irene."

Father Thomas nodded thoughtfully. "Marko, Father Nestor tells me that he is taking you with him to Ierissos. You have family there?"

Marko nodded.

"I would like you to write a letter to your parents, telling them where you are going, and leave it with me. If we happen upon any word of them, I will be able to tell them where you are. And we will keep all of you in our continual prayers that you arrive safely at your destination and are reunited."

Marko thanked him and left the room, but before he was down the hall, he heard Father Thomas ask, "Why did you bring the icon with you off of Rhodes?"

Marko stopped in his tracks.

"Surely it would have been wiser to leave such a holy item in its home," Father Thomas continued.

"The island fell to invaders," Father Nestor pointed out. "But besides that, Marko is hurting. There is a wound deep within him that only God can reach. And his face, when he first saw the icon . . ." His voice trailed off. There was a long pause before Father Nestor continued. "When I saw him drawn to the saint as he was, I felt a nudge, a whisper from the Holy Spirit that the two of them should not be separated. I couldn't ignore it, even if I don't understand."

Marko heard Father Thomas murmur a reply, but he did not linger to hear more. Returning to his room, he wrote the brief letter and then spent the afternoon work-ing in the monastery orchard, picking lemons for the kitchen and pondering Father Nestor's revelation. After the evening meal and vespers, Father Nestor caught up with Marko.

"Father Thomas has made arrangements for us on a ship bound for Athens. From there, we will be able to book passage to Athos."

A surge of wild hope, mingled with terror, reared up in Marko's chest. "When?" he stammered.

"Our ship leaves in a few days, but Father Thomas sends one of his monks every few weeks with correspondence to other monasteries and churches on Crete. He has included a note about your family with the monk who left this afternoon, telling them where we are headed. If your parents have stopped on Crete at any of the monasteries, they will know where to find you."

That night as he lay in bed, he looked at the icon, which had been returned to his room. A single *lampada* burned in front of it. Marko said a small, halting prayer and curled in a ball to sleep.

THE WIND WHIPPED Marko's already wild hair into a frenzy as the ship picked up speed. Crete disappeared behind them, and two days' sailing would bring them to Athens. He rested his forearms on the ship's rail and looked ahead. The clear blue water stretched out as far as he could see, the swells crashing against the ship's hull echoing the storm in his mind.

Father Nestor found him looking out over the waves. "Father Ignatios and I have been asking among the other passengers, but it is the same as everywhere else. No one seems to have heard of our Saint Phanourios."

"It seems so strange that such a great martyr would be unknown to everyone," Marko commented.

"I agree," Father Nestor admitted. "But all we can do is keep asking. There are monks and priests and bishops in the world who are far more educated than I am. When we arrive at Athos, surely someone will have answers. But even if they don't, we will keep Father Thomas's words in mind. It is enough that we know Saint Phanourios existed. We will continue to pray and give thanks to God for His many mercies—like the fact that, unlike our last sea voyage, there is food for us this time!"

Marko agreed, hoping that he would never again have to endure the starvation of Rhodes.

"How is Father Kosmas?" The last time Marko had seen him, the young monk's ruddy face had been a peculiar shade of green.

"Surviving," Father Nestor said wryly. "He slept most of the last voyage. And now that his belly isn't empty, well, it's a different story." The older monk exhaled a deep, contented breath. "Tell me about your home, Marko."

Marko was thoughtful. He told Father Nestor about his friend Makarios, how they competed against each other in their small, one-room schoolhouse, attempted to climb the stone wall of Rhodes, and played games in the trees and in the clear blue water surrounding their island. He even recounted the time they had accidentally started a small censer fire on Pascha, while they sleepily served as acolytes. Marko glanced sideways at Father Nestor as he told that particular story, and Father Nestor responded by shaking back his cassock sleeve to show Marko a series of burns from his own censer mishap.

He talked about his goats and the excitement of waking up one morning to find babies in the barn with their mothers, and he wistfully described his own mother's cooking. Father Nestor nodded and asked questions, chuckling as Marko described the difficulties of sleeping in the hay with a half-grown goat.

"All those nights with the goats," Father Nestor said thoughtfully. "My goodness, you must have smelled interesting in the morning."

Marko instinctively bent his nose to his shoulder and sniffed. "No animals here," Father Nestor chuckled.

"Only Father Kosmas," Marko said without thinking, and froze in horror. He turned slowly to look at Father Nestor, and found the older monk choking on his surprised laughter. Marko relaxed and looked out at the ocean.

There was nothing to see, just the endless rolling waves, capped with white foam, but then the water parted. He heard a *whoosh* of expelled air that shot droplets of seawater as high as the deck, and a hulking gray mass appeared above the waves. Marko caught his breath and held completely still. The behemoth rolled slightly to one side, revealing a single, huge eye larger than Marko's entire face. It blinked once and sank silently beneath the surface, the waves covering its exit as though it had never been there at all.

Marko's shock cemented him in place, his knuckles white as he gripped the railing. He released his breath in a great puff and blinked several times, not entirely sure if his imagination had created the encounter or if that great animal was still there, lurking in the dark water alongside the ship. He glanced to his side. Father Nestor's mouth hung open, and he stared dumbly at the water lapping gently on the wooden bulkhead in the exact place where Marko had seen the . . . ? Not a hallucination, then.

The abbot had astonishment written all over his face. A nervous laugh escaped Marko's lips, but the monk was lost in thought. He met Marko's eye, and the side of his mouth pulled upwards as he quoted, "'Thus God made great sea creatures and every living thing that moves with which the waters abounded, according to their kind, and . . . God saw that it was good.'" Father Nestor's face had relaxed, and he remarked, "I always wondered what the Bible meant by 'great sea creatures.'"

Marko was speechless. The ramifications of that particular biblical description had never occurred to him. It was just a reading, one of hundreds that he had heard in services throughout the course of the church year. Now questions flooded his mind. Did God's declaration that the creation was good mean it was friendly? Or were they in danger of that creation taking a bite out of the side of the boat? What else lived and swam in the dark depths that surrounded them? He had a sudden vision of great tentacles and large teeth and was contemplating the wisdom of panic when he realized Father Nestor was speaking.

"I'm sorry, what did you say?"

"I said," Father Nestor repeated, taking up the same position as Marko, his arms on the railing as he looked out over the water, "that this water makes me think of the Sea of Galilee."

Marko furrowed his eyebrows in confusion and tilted his head. "Galilee?"

"In the Gospel of Matthew. It is where Jesus walked on water out to His disciples during the storm."

"I didn't know Jesus lived on the ocean," was all Marko could think of to say.

"Jesus sent his disciples out in a boat ahead of him, but there was a large storm, and the boat was in danger. The disciples spent all night in the boat, trying to cross to the other side, and just before morning they saw what they thought was a ghost. Do you remember this story?"

Marko nodded. "It was Jesus, and He walked on the water."

"Yes. And what happened next?"

Marko closed one eye tightly and tilted his head. "Didn't Peter get out of the boat?"

Father Nestor smiled. "He did. But first he tested Jesus, saying, 'Lord, if it is You, command me to come to You on the water.' So Jesus told him to come. And Peter did. But when he saw the wind and the waves, he grew fearful, and he began to sink. So he cried out to Jesus to save him, and Jesus reached out His hand and caught Peter."

Marko looked out at the cloudless sky and the gentle waves propelling them forward. "And this ocean reminds you of that?"

Father Nestor nodded. "Yes, and of you."

"Me?" Marko was taken aback.

"All that has happened to you: your brother's death and all the grief and pain that followed, war, being separated from your parents, starvation, sea journeys. . . . Does that not sound like a storm to you?"

Marko swallowed hard past the lump in his throat and the hurt in his chest.

"God has not abandoned you, Marko. This is your moment to learn from Peter's mistake. He took his eyes off the Lord and saw only the waves."

The pain in Marko's chest sharpened into a single point.

"Your storm is great, Marko," Father Nestor whispered. "But our God is greater."

CHAPTER 18

By the second morning at sea, Father Kosmas's shade of green had deepened to an alarming hue.

"I thought you worked on boats," Marko said as the monk watched him inhale his breakfast.

"A harbor, Marko. I worked in a harbor. And I was around your age, too. Taller, though," he added.

"You were eleven?" Marko asked in surprise around a mouthful of bread, and several crumbs sprayed out with his response. He swallowed quickly, intending to clarify his odd statement, but the bread was dry and caught in his throat. After a minor coughing fit, during which Father Ignatios pounded him several times on the back, he swallowed successfully, took a deep breath, and explained, "I mean, you worked in a harbor when you were eleven?"

"Close. I was thirteen. My brother and I ran away to be sailors, but the first day at sea I discovered that I had no stomach for the ocean." Father Kosmas grimaced at the bread Marko offered and waved his hand in refusal. "The ship's captain was a hard man and had no use for a seasick child, so he dropped me at the first port we came to, which was Kos, on the mainland. On a clear day, you can actually see Rhodes from the beach."

"He just left you there?" Marko demanded in outrage.

"He did. The other boat captains would only take me on if I could work, but since I get so seasick, that wasn't a possibility. I had no money. The harbormaster eventually took pity on me and brought me to his house. He had a son my age, and I was his servant. I attended classes with him, and that is where I discovered I had a talent for languages. Omar—the harbormaster—took me to work with him, translating for the ships that came in."

"How did you get back to Rhodes?"

Father Kosmas held a clenched fist up to his mouth and shook his head gingerly. "Another time, Marko." He glanced out at the rolling waves. "Hopefully when we're on land."

A storm kept them from making port in Athens, and

they were forced to spend an extra two days at the mercy of the raging sea. Marko did his best to distract Father Kosmas but began to wonder if a person could actually die of seasickness. Father Nestor assured him that no one ever had, but Marko had his doubts and hoped that Father Kosmas wouldn't be the first.

When they finally disembarked in Athens, there were no ships leaving for another two days. Father Nestor declared this circumstance a gift from God, stating that Father Kosmas needed to recover, eat, and regain his strength. They booked passage and spent the two days waiting at the church of Agios Pavlos, where the kind *presbytera* fussed over them, insisting on washing their travel-stained clothes and feeding them until their stomachs ached. Under her motherly eye, Father Kosmas lost his seasick pallor and began to walk steadily again.

Father Ignatios and Father Nestor left Father Kosmas to rest and spent their time circulating among the churches in Athens. They asked after Iakovos and Eleni and tried unsuccessfully to find someone—anyone—who could tell them more about Saint Phanourios.

Marko was eating his second helping of baklava at Presbytera Anastasia's kitchen table when Father Nestor burst through the door. The smile on his face was so large that Marko was momentarily taken aback. "Marko!" he shouted in triumph. "We have word of your parents!"

Marko choked on his pastry. "They're here?" he asked between coughs.

Father Nestor pounded on his back and then poured him a glass of water. "No, they did not stay. But Father Vasili from the Church of the Holy Transfiguration met them and put them on a ship traveling north two weeks ago. And, as we are headed north also, we can only assume that, by God's grace, they are going to your aunt in Ierissos, and we will find them there."

Marko looked around the kitchen wildly, every muscle in his body tensed for instant action. "What do we do?" he asked frantically.

Father Nestor laughed. "First, we give thanks to God for all things! Glory to Jesus Christ!"

"Glory forever!" Presbytera Anastasia shouted from the next room. Marko barked a single surprised laugh at her automatic response. He bounced in place, overcome with sudden excitement. "Glory forever," he echoed, tentatively attempting his own simple prayer of thanksgiving.

"Now, get yourself outside and run off some of that energy, because you need to sleep tonight. Our ship leaves at dawn." Father Nestor opened the door and pointed. Marko grinned and stuffed the last half of his baklava in his mouth before heading out into the sunlit afternoon.

He spent the rest of the day running wild with a pack of neighborhood boys, climbing trees and kicking a ball made of rags. He was dirty and bruised and possessed a dozen scratches from playing. He came back inside when darkness fell, and Presbytera fussed over him, washing the scratches and making clucking noises over the scar on his forehead. She attacked his unruly hair with a comb, attempting to subdue it with water and admonition. When she was satisfied that he was clean and whole, he helped her milk their goat and put her chickens in for the night.

She had spent the day cooking, aghast at their thinness, and fed Marko and the monks roasted lamb, tzatziki and moussaka, declaring the news of Marko's family worthy of a feast. The weight of his full belly rested comfortably under a hopeful heart, and Marko's eyelids grew heavier. "Thank You, God, for this day," he prayed, and the same peace that he had felt earlier warmed in his chest. Marko yawned drowsily, giving in at last to sleep.

Father Ignatios shook him awake before the sun rose, and Marko dressed sluggishly in the darkness, rubbing his bleary eyes as he stumbled to the front door. Presbytera Anastasia hugged him fiercely and pressed a large cloth sack in his hands. "You tell your mama what a wonderful young man she has," she told him with a stern voice that was betrayed by the twinkle in her eye. "I put a present in there. Give it to your mama when you see her."

He felt a sudden surge of gratefulness, and without thinking, Marko threw his arms around her. Presbytera chuckled and patted his tangled hair. "You look better today, Marko. You are eleven again, instead of eighty. Try and stay that way."

Marko grinned. "I promise." The monks waited for him on the edge of the cobblestone street, and he ran to catch up. He stumbled over a large shape and was astonished when it honked at him. Presbytera Anastasia had closed the door but threw it open again at the sound of turmoil in her front yard, illuminating the scene with candlelight from the house.

Marko had fallen on his back and was alarmed to see one of the neighbor's evil-tempered geese standing over him, its wings outstretched and rounded beak ready to strike. He scuttled backward, avoiding the first peck as the goose hissed at him, undeterred, and waddled angrily to attack again.

Presbytera wasted no time. Before the goose had a chance to inflict injury, she beat it over the head with a broom. The goose squawked in indignation but abandoned its pursuit of Marko, weaving a drunken pattern in the opposite direction. Marko allowed his rescuer to pull him up, dust the dirt off his clothes, and give a second final parting hug before she closed the door, dousing the yard back into darkness.

He gingerly navigated the last few steps across the yard, listening warily for the sounds of any other angry fowl hidden in the shadows. He heard nothing except for a fizzing noise that seemed to be emanating from Father Ignatios. His eyes slowly adjusted to the dimness, and he saw that all three of the monks were shaking with the effort of suppressed laughter.

"Um, sorry I took so long," he mumbled in embarrassment. Father Kosmas lost his battle and whooped out loud, clapping a hand over his mouth as Father Ignatios elbowed him sharply in the ribs. Marko was thoroughly embarrassed, but he recalled the sight of the tiny presbytera attacking the cranky bird with a broom, and he chuckled in spite of himself. He hoped to remember that particular image forever.

The monks exchanged fond glances. "No apologies, Marko," Father Ignatios said. "It is good to see you smiling."

They boarded the ship in the early morning darkness, settling with practiced ease on the deck among barrels and crates. Marko curled up on a broad lid to watch the sun rise as the ship cast off. Father Kosmas groaned.

Their captain was a busy man, but friendly. He had

children of his own, and in their absence he used his bits of spare time to get to know Marko. He showed him the map that they followed, tracing a finger along the channels and isthmus that formed the outline of Greece. Their course hugged the coast, meandering slowly north around bays and peninsulas before taking an abrupt right turn to the east, down a finger of land that housed Athos at its end.

They made several stops to discharge cargo along the way. In each city, they waited at the end of the long, slow line to disembark in order to find fresh food for the coming days. Other passengers came and went, and their group of traveling companions changed so frequently that Marko stopped trying to remember them. Father Kosmas, permanently green and noticeably thinner, was given special permission by the captain to skip the lines and be the first off the ship. He would collapse on the wharf and wait for his stomach to settle, and, once able, he would eat slowly, filling his belly enough, he hoped, to tide him over to the next stop. When it was time to leave again, he waited patiently until it was time to cast off before reluctantly climbing back aboard.

The days blurred together. The monks took refuge in their prayer ropes, saying the Jesus Prayer quietly under their breath, the sound a comforting backdrop as Marko watched the waves and dozed. Father Kosmas shared more of his story in fits and spurts, about how his brother had rescued him from Kos years later and how he had made it back to Rhodes, and of his first visit to the monastery. "I never left," he said simply, shrugging his wide shoulders. "It was home."

"I love the sea," Father Kosmas told him later. "But it does not love me." Marko was beginning to agree. He was tired of ships and eager to find his family. Father Nestor's quiet assurances of their love had lit a tiny flame of hope inside of him, and his fears began to soften. He realized one day that he hadn't had a nightmare in days, and Father Ignatios smiled softly each time he laughed.

He received permission to unwrap the icon of Saint Phanourios at his leisure and spent many of his waking hours studying the story of the saint's martyrdom depicted around the edges. "Who are you?" Marko asked him every day. The saint never replied in words, but Marko could feel the connection between them. He grew bolder in his prayers, hanging on with both hands to the peace growing inside. "I hope we both find our homes," Marko whispered late one night, as the boat rocked him to sleep.

The ship docked again the next evening at another port, which looked exactly the same as every other small town they had seen. Marko grumpily stumbled to his feet, feeling queasy after the seemingly endless days on the water. "Where are we now?" he wearily asked Father Ignatios, who grinned and gestured with an open hand.

"Ierissos."

CHAPTER 19

"We're here," Marko whispered, his voice hoarse. A burning fear suddenly lit in his chest, and a thousand thoughts blurred through his mind. What if they weren't here? What if they were? What if—he swallowed painfully—what if they weren't happy to see him?

"Courage, Marko," Father Nestor said, seeing the panic rise in Marko's face. "Come here, and we will pray together."

Marko huddled together with the monks who had become his second family, reassured by their presence. Father Nestor prayed fervently, giving thanks for their safety thus far, and asked for God's reassurance and peace to ease Marko's fears. Finally, he said a special prayer, asking the Theotokos, the angels, and all the saints for a joyful reunion with his mother and father.

"Especially Saint Phanourios," Marko added in a rush.

"And especially Saint Phanourios," Father Nestor agreed. "Please grant us divine assistance in our search. Amen."

Disembarking, always a slow and convoluted process, took an eternity as Marko bounced from one foot to the other, a ball of nervous energy. "God, help me," he whispered over and over again. "Saint Phanourios, I am so afraid."

Marko's anxiety twisted into nausea as the wait continued. Father Nestor looked at him sharply as Marko shivered in the hot sun.

"Marko." He waved his prayer rope through the air for attention. Marko looked at him wildly. "Remember the Sea of Galilee."

"The Sea of Galilee," Marko repeated.

"Keep your eyes on Jesus."

"On Jesus," Marko said, taking a deep breath. He envisioned Jesus reaching out to him.

"Remember, your storm is great."

"But our God is greater," Marko finished. He breathed in and out, praying slowly as each breath passed his lips, and then it was his turn on the gangplank. He had to force himself to walk and not take off running.

He was only half listening to the conversation around him when Father Nestor said, "Marko, we will have to start searching tomorrow. It is late, and we must find a place to sleep."

Marko nodded, enough emotions warring within him that he barely had the focus to do even that. A family that Father Ignatios had befriended on the boat took pity on them and opened their home to the four travelers. Marko was torn between wanting to sleep and put off tomorrow forever, and running up and down the dark streets, banging on doors until he found his aunt. Father Nestor sensed his struggle and planted him firmly in a chair. "Tomorrow, Marko. Rest and pray, and we will face our problems in the morning."

"I don't think that I can." Marko ran both hands over his head in frustration, leaving his dark hair standing upright.

"Pray for peace," Father Ignatios said, passing Marko his prayer rope. The knots were smooth, the woolen threads worn down by the monk's many prayers. "You may borrow it for tonight."

Marko was certain that he would never be able to sleep. He lay on his pallet on the kitchen floor, clutching Father Ignatios's prayer rope and attempting to pray. He quickly gave up on his own words and listened instead to Father Kosmas's whispered psalm beside him. "'Oh God, my God, I rise early to be with You; my soul thirsts for You. How often my flesh thirsts for You in a desolate, impassable, and waterless land. . . .'"

Marko closed his eyes briefly, and when he opened them, he was shocked to find that morning had arrived. He lay still for a moment, watching the dust motes dance in the sunlight. As the fog cleared from his brain, he suddenly remembered where he was. Energy surged through his muscles, and he sat bolt upright.

He heard a chuckle nearby and saw Father Kosmas, his normal ruddy skin tone restored, chewing on a piece of fruit. "What time is it?" Marko demanded.

"If you're awake, it's time to go searching for your aunt," Father Nestor responded, poking his head into the room. He scrutinized Marko for a brief moment and said, "But perhaps we can wait long enough for you to brush your hair."

"Marko," Father Ignatios asked a few moments later as he pulled on his shoes, "do you know where your aunt lives?"

Marko stopped in his tracks, shocked into stillness. "No. Oh, no. How will we find her?"

"Don't worry," Father Nestor said. "We will find a church and ask the priest for help."

"Why do we always start at the church? Why not the market or the shops?" Marko asked.

"It's a good life lesson, Marko," Father Nestor said firmly. "Always start with the church. Everything else will fall into place." He had a hurried conversation with their host about local churches while Marko pawed frantically at his wild hair, bouncing from one foot to the other. He declined the offer of breakfast, his stomach too twisted with nerves to eat. Gnawing on his fingernail, he squirmed in place as the monks made plans. Finally reaching a consensus, they bid their hosts farewell and headed down the street.

The parish of Saint Nicholas was their first stop, and when the blue domed church came into view, Marko stopped abruptly and reached blindly to grab the arm of the cassock nearest him. He didn't know which monk crushed him in a fierce embrace; he simply stood until the trembling stopped, listening to a murmur in his ear that made no sense but that he knew was prayer.

Two hands gripped his shoulders and forced him back a step so that Marko could see the face of Father Ignatios. "We are with you, Marko, and we will stay with you as long as you need. But God is also with you, and He will never leave you. Do not be afraid."

"For I am with you," Marko whispered. Father Nestor blessed him, thumping his forehead gently with twisted fingers as he drew a firm cross over him. Marko allowed himself to be led by the elbow down the street and into the church. With each step, Marko prayed, "Saint Phanourios, please help me find my courage."

The priest at Saint Nicholas had not heard of Marko's Aunt Diana, so they thanked him and continued their way through the city. They had a similar experience at Saint

Paul's and again at Saint Panteleimon's. Marko began to despair.

They stopped for a meal at a street vendor who was selling lamb kebabs, and Marko stared for a long moment at the skewer in his hands before gnawing on the end. The rich spice of the hot meat filled his mouth and reminded him exactly how hungry he was. He finished in three bites, and the vendor winked and handed him a second. Marko smiled his thanks and tried to take smaller bites to make the food last longer. He was partially successful.

They heard the clanging of nearby bells, calling the faithful to vespers. "What church is that?" Father Ignatios asked the vendor.

"Ekklesia Panagia," the man replied. "The Church of the Theotokos, my own home church." He pointed down a side street and gave directions before asking Father Nestor's blessing and turning to help new customers.

They followed the haphazard directions, getting lost once and slightly turned around another time before reaching the church. "I think we've missed vespers," Father Kosmas said as the church doors were flung open and the congregation began to spill out. Marko's response was lost in the sudden chatter of the crowd. He followed the monks to the side of the small lawn to wait until the people had dispersed.

In later years, when he tried to tell the story of what happened next, he was never quite able to put his finger on the exact events. He stood a little way off from the monks, not paying attention as they quietly made plans. A soft breeze ruffled his hair, and Marko realized that he no longer felt alone. A voice whispered, "Look there," and Marko never knew if he heard it in his ears or in his heart, but he listened, and he looked.

At first he could see only their backs. The woman wore a brightly colored scarf wrapped around her dark hair, and she had her hand tucked in the arm of the tall man beside her. His other hand held tightly to a young girl skipping at her father's side. She tugged at the man's hand, pulling him to a stop. He conceded with a smile, and the girl bent to pick a small bunch of wildflowers from the edge of the churchyard.

Marko was frozen to the spot, as though his feet had

turned to roots and planted him as firmly as an olive tree in the ground. He inhaled a ragged gasp of breath. Father Ignatios looked up in alarm and followed his gaze.

It was then that the woman turned her head and looked behind her. Everything around him ceased—the birds, the sun, the worry, the pain, and perhaps time itself stopped because at that moment, there was nothing else in the entire world except for the sight of his mother's face and the sound of her voice crying out his name.

And then the roots were gone; he was free of the weight that had grounded him, and he was running faster than he had ever run before, gasping for breath, headlong through the crowd. Mama met him in a thunderclap of an embrace, and they collapsed in a heap on the ground, her arms wrapped around him as she sobbed into his hair. Then his father was there, wrapped around them both, his strong arms familiar and comforting, and Irene was at his side with her face buried in his shoulder. "Papa, Mama," he gasped, "I'm so sorry."

"Sorry?" Papa exclaimed in shock. "Marko, what on earth for?"

"Elias." Marko tried to pull away, but Mama would not let him go. "Oh, Marko," she whispered, and she cupped his face in her hands, bending her forehead to touch his. Marko looked from her eyes to his father's, and he saw in them the love and forgiveness he had been too afraid to look for since the day his brother died. Relief surged through him in great waves as his muscles released the strain and agony that they had carried for far too long. He slumped to the ground and shuddered great sobs, supported by his father's arms and his mother's embrace, and as his family's tears mingled with his own, he knew he was home.

Marko never knew how long they clung together on the grass in front of the church. It may have been hours, or perhaps it was several wonderful and sunlit days, but he cried until all his tears, saved from the day he had carried Elias home until this moment, were spent. His mother lifted her cheek off of Marko's head and looked into his eyes.

"My son," she said quietly, tears creeping back into her eyes. "I am so very glad to see you."

"Mama," he choked. "I was so afraid. I thought you would hate me, and then I thought I would never find you." She made several soothing noises and clutched him tightly to her again.

Marko gradually became aware of the monks nearby, who were weeping joyfully and glorifying God as they watched the family reunite. Marko clambered to his feet, still holding tight to his parents, and introduced them. Eleni clasped each of the monks' hands with both of hers, taking special, gentle care with Father Nestor's, and thanked them, again and again, for bringing Marko home to them.

"We are honored and privileged to have had the care of him," Father Nestor said, emotion thick in his voice. "We are so grateful to God for reuniting you." Then he turned to Marko with a twinkle in his green eyes and said, "What did I tell you, Marko? Always start with the church."

CHAPTER 20

IT WAS LATE IN THE EVENING. All the stories had been told, the tears had been cried again, and Marko sat with his family and the monks in his aunt's living room. His grandparents, who had also fled safely from Rhodes, had kissed him goodbye and left for their own small home nearby.

"What a journey," Iakovos said, for perhaps the eighth time.

"Thank God, we survived it, and now it is over. For Marko at least," replied Father Ignatios, smiling at Marko, who was ensconced between his parents and showed no sign of ever wanting to move. "In the morning, we will take the ferry to the Holy Mountain. Saint Phanourios will be returned to a church, and we will live there until things have settled at home."

"Our hope," Father Nestor added, his face soft with

emotion, "is to eventually return to Rhodes. We would like to return Saint Phanourios home as well. Since his church was raided, perhaps we will build him a new one."

"I wish you didn't have to go," Marko said sadly.

Father Nestor smiled. "We are monks, Marko, and monks belong in monasteries. We will send you word when we have settled, and you can visit us."

Marko nodded. He felt selfish; today all his prayers had been answered, and he still wished the monks didn't have to leave. Father Ignatios seemed to understand his struggle and told him fondly, "We will miss you as well."

Marko remembered with a start the bag that Presbytera Anastasia had entrusted to him in Athens. Mostly it had been full of fruit and sweet pastries, which he had long since finished, but there was a brown paper package wrapped at the bottom for his mother. Rummaging through his meager belongings, he found it, explaining its origins to her. She unwrapped the package, and the smells wafted out as the first layers were undone.

Eleni gasped in delight as carefully wrapped spices spilled into her lap. Rare and expensive cinnamon, cloves, and even exotic cardamom pods filled the room with their fragrance. "What a gift," she said in awe. They passed the package around the room, each taking a moment to inhale the heady scents before passing them on. When they had made their way back to Eleni, she wrapped them and smiled at the assembly.

Marko found something else in the depths of his bag. With a shy smile, he showed everyone the bundle he had carefully wrapped before leaving his childhood home for the last time. Irene smiled wistfully at the rooster feather and ran her hands along the softness. "Aunt Diana says that I can have the next batch of chicks that hatches," she informed Marko. He smiled back at her and pulled her into a one-armed hug.

Mama was crying again, the scarf that Marko had carried across so many miles held tightly in her hands. "Marko," she whispered. She smiled through her tears and pressed a firm kiss over the scar on his forehead. The scarf unwrapped, and a piece of discolored and battered parchment fluttered to the ground. Mama gasped. "Is that . . . ?"

Marko nodded. "A man brought this letter to our house for you," he told Papa. "He said it was urgent, and that's why I left to find you. But I got lost, and then the fighting . . ."

Papa nodded. "I wonder what was so important?" He carefully unfolded the paper and scanned the spidery black writing. His eyes widened, and he burst into laughter. He handed the letter to Mama, and as she read it, her mouth formed a large "O."

"What is it?" Marko demanded.

Papa took the letter back and read aloud in a voice shaking with mirth. "'Dear Sir. My neighbor has stolen my wife's apron and my favorite shovel. Please send troops immediately to retrieve my belongings.'"

"What?" Marko wasn't sure he had heard correctly. Papa was rolling with laughter.

"He said it was important!" Marko cried indignantly.

Papa fanned his face with the letter, still chuckling. Father Kosmas looked at them all and said dryly, "He must have really loved that shovel."

When the laughter died away, Mama looked at the

monks. "Will you delay your journey to the Holy Mountain for another day?" she asked. "I would like the opportunity to gift you with one small thing tomorrow as a thank-you."

They looked at each other and nodded. "Father Kosmas will do anything to stay off a boat," Marko said through a yawn.

Father Kosmas whooped with laughter. "And don't you forget it!"

Marko wanted his bed, the simple blanket-covered pallet in his aunt's spare room where his whole family was staying until they found a home of their own. He thought it sounded like heaven.

"Since you are staying until tomorrow," Marko said as he paused on his way out of the room, "may I keep Saint Phanourios with me this last night?"

They all looked to the icon corner, where the large, unwrapped icon stood on a stool in a place of honor. It had survived the long and arduous journey without a blemish. The monks and Marko had shared the tale of its discovery in the church and the increasing mystery surrounding the saint and his history. Marko had told quietly of his connection to Saint Phanourios, causing his mother to weep again as he described them both as being lost. "But lost no more," he had concluded. "At least I'm not."

Father Ignatios made a *metania* before Saint Phanourios. He handed the icon to Marko, who kissed the saint's hand and carried it to his room. Placing the icon on a chair in the corner, where Saint Phanourios could keep watch over his whole family, he prayed out loud the prayer that had been singing in his heart for hours. "Thank you, Saint Phanourios. Thank you for finding my family."

When Marko fell asleep that night, it was with his sister pressed up against his side, his mother's hand in his, and joy in his heart.

CHAPTER 21

MARKO STUMBLED INTO the kitchen early, finding only his mother and Irene awake. Mama hugged him closely for a long moment, then planted a kiss on his forehead and put a hard-boiled egg in his hand.

"Eat," she commanded. "You have lost too much weight."

"Yes, Mama," Marko said, grinning.

She wagged a finger at him. "Don't laugh at your mother," she said sternly, her own laughter held barely in check. Marko hugged her again and sat at the table to peel his still-warm egg.

Eleni moved gracefully through the kitchen, her long skirts swishing against her legs as she gathered ingredients. She pulled a brightly colored pottery bowl from the shelf, and Marko was startled to see that it was the bowl he had given her. He had not noticed its absence when he was briefly home with the monks. Mama patted the bowl fondly and smiled. "You didn't think I would leave it behind, did you?"

Marko returned her smile, and it grew broader as she began to hum. Into the bowl went flour, honey, and salt. She carefully grated one of the precious cinnamon sticks from Presbytera Anastasia into a fine powder. The spicy scent filled the kitchen.

"Marko, run out to your aunt's garden. Pick me four big, heavy oranges." Marko stood to obey, and as he passed his mother on his way to the kitchen door, she pressed another kiss on his head and another egg in his hand. Irene followed close behind, skipping at his side as he took a deep breath of the early morning air.

The sun was just peeking over the horizon. Bright streaks of light filled the eastern sky. In the hazy light, Marko recognized olive, lemon, and lime before he reached the orange tree, its branches heavy with fruit. The clean, fresh smell of citrus permeated the air. Marko ate his egg in two bites and reached into the heavily laden branches. He picked a dozen oranges, each the size of his fist. Irene carried some in her apron, and Marko untucked his shirt to form a bag to carry the rest.

Reentering the kitchen, his mother scolded them. "I only need four!"

Marko spilled his oranges onto the table. "I'm going to eat the rest."

Eleni smiled. "Well, in that case, pick twenty."

Marko slowly peeled an orange as he watched his mother squeeze the juice out of the four largest, mixing it with the batter and several glugs of rich green olive oil. The many smells of the kitchen all competed for his attention, and Marko sat back and started on his second orange as Eleni scraped the thick dough into a baking pan and slid it into the warm oven.

"Mama, what are you making?" he asked around bites.

"A cake."

"Why?" Eleni raised her eyebrows at him and he hurried to add, "I love cake, but I was just wondering why you were up so early to start this one."

Eleni smiled. "Because my lost son is found. You are certainly no prodigal, but we will eat, drink, and be merry.

And since I have no fatted calf to kill"—a goat bleated indignantly in the yard, making them both chuckle—"I will bake a cake instead, using the beautiful gifts from Presbytera Anastasia. And we will share it with our family and our new friends as we make a fresh start here." She reached over and scooped the rest of the oranges into a bowl. "No more, Marko, you'll make yourself sick. Have a cookie instead."

The rising sun and the sweet smell of baking cake soon pulled the rest of the household from their beds. Eleni and her sister flew to prepare breakfast for the small crowd. When the morning work was done, they gathered for slices of the now cooled cake. Several neighbors, having witnessed the reunion in front of the church, stopped by with gifts to welcome Marko. They sat and listened as he and the monks told the story again and again of their journey, and they stopped to venerate the icon of Saint Phanourios as they left. The house was full all afternoon, and Eleni kept slicing slivers of cake, but it never ran out. "Like the loaves and fishes," Iakovos commented with a kiss on her cheek.

The monks declined supper, packing their small bags and preparing to catch the last ferry of the day to Athos. "It's a very short ride," Iakovos told Father Kosmas, who nodded grimly but winked at Marko.

He and his family lined up to venerate Saint Phanourios one last time before the monks carefully wrapped the icon for the final leg of their journey. Marko kissed the saint's hand, leaning his forehead briefly against the icon as he whispered, "Thank you."

His goodbyes to the monks were full of joyful sorrow. Father Nestor blessed and hugged him in turn, and Father Kosmas wrapped his thick arms around Marko, lifting his feet off the ground in an enormous embrace. Father Ignatios was last, and he pressed his own worn prayer rope into Marko's hand. "Keep this, and use it well," he said. "We will pray for you always."

Marko smiled as best he could. He was saddened to say goodbye to the monks who had become his friends and brothers, but the feel of his mother's arm around his waist and Irene's hand in in his dispelled his grief. He had cried enough.

As the ferry pushed off from the dock, Marko waved at the monks. They waved back, Father Kosmas's wild hair visible even at a distance. Before they were out of range, Marko saw Father Nestor cup his twisted hands around his mouth and call, "Marko! Your storm is great!"

Marko shouted back with all his might, "But our God is greater!"

That night as they prepared for bed, Marko thought over all that he had found. Not just his family, but new friends, forgiveness, faith, and the courage that had been granted to him all along the journey. Father Nestor was right. His storm had been great. But now, just like he did for the apostles on the Sea of Galilee, Christ had calmed the wind and the waves and left him with peace.

Marko helped carry the last of their belongings into the new house. He wore the new breeches Eleni had stayed up late to sew, his other two pairs ripped and worn through with the turmoil of hard travel. The neighbors had gifted his family with furniture for the rooms and pots for the kitchen, and his mother was tilling up ground in the backyard to start a garden. He would have to remember to save some seeds from his aunt's oranges so they could have their own trees in a few years. In the meantime, he was happy to run the short distance with a basket to pick fruit and olives.

"Marko?" asked Irene. "Have you seen the milk pail? I can't find it."

"Say a prayer and ask Saint Phanourios to help you."

Irene wrinkled her nose. "That seems funny, asking a saint to help you find something."

Marko tossed an orange to his sister. "He helped me find you, didn't he?"

Irene smiled. "Yes, I suppose he did. I will pray."

"Good," Marko winked. "And when you find it, let's see if Mama will bake another cake."

THE END

FROM THE AUTHOR

THE MYSTERY OF SAINT PHANOURIOS is a real one that has baffled Orthodox faithful for over five hundred years. It's commonly believed that during the second Siege of Rhodes in 1522, several monks watched a group of enemy soldiers raid a church. When the soldiers left, the monks found the icon of Saint Phanourios buried in a heap of old and discarded icons, looking perfect and new.

The monks searched far and wide for the story of the mysterious saint, but none has ever been found. A bishop who later saw the icon declared that it was enough that the icon existed, that either someone knew his story or that the icon was created miraculously and left for the monks to find. The bishop canonized Saint Phanourios, and his feast day, August 27, is the day that his icon was discovered.

We don't know the real names of the monks who found the icon of Saint Phanourios, so in my mind, they became Fathers Kosmas, Ignatios, and Nestor. I wondered what it would have been like to be a young person watching that discovery, and so I created Marko to be another witness along with the monks. His struggles with grief and loss are shared by many throughout the ages.

Saint Phanourios is the patron saint of lost things. Since his history is lost, but he himself was found, we pray to him when we need help finding something. The prayer can be as simple as "Saint Phanourios, help me!" It is traditional to bake a special cake, called a Fanouropita (Saint Phanourios Cake), in thanks. We don't know how this tradition began, but it is practiced all over the world.

The icon of Saint Phanourios was found within the city of Rhodes, Greece. The wall that surrounded Rhodes back in the 1500s, and that protected it for many years, still stands today, but the city has grown over the centuries and now exists outside the original boundaries. Today, the icon of Saint Phanourios resides in a church dedicated to the saint, which sits on top of the original site where it was discovered.

The mystery of his past may never be uncovered, but Saint Phanourios continually answers the prayers of those lost and seeking his help. Holy Saint Phanourios, pray to God for us!

TROPARION TO

Saint Phanourios

A heavenly song of praise is chanted radiantly upon the earth

the company of angels now joyfully celebrates an earthly festival,

and from on high with hymns they praise your contests,

and from below, the church proclaims the heavenly glory

which you have found by your labors and struggles,

O GLORIOUS PHANOURIUS.

KONTAKION TO

Saint Phanourios

You saved the priests from an ungodly captivity,

and broke their bonds by divine power, O godly-minded one;

you bravely put to shame the audacity of the tyrants,

and made glad the orders of the angels, O great martyr.

Therefore, we honor you,

O DIVINE WARRIOR, GLORIOUS PHANOURIUS.

Icon image from OrthodoxWiki.org
Icon of Saint Phanourios, from Rhodes, Greece.

Saint Phanourios Cake

FANOUROPITA

THIS IS A MODERN RECIPE. Marko's mother would not have had baking soda, or perhaps even sugar. Mostly likely, she would have sweetened her cakes with honey, as that would have been more readily available.

In order to make this recipe without eggs, you could substitute ¾ cup of fruit puree (banana, unsweetened applesauce, or even avocado) for the three eggs. The texture of the cake will change a little if you choose to make the swap.

Enjoy, and may Saint Phanourios intercede for all of us!

INGREDIENTS

3 eggs

I cup sugar, plus 2 tablespoons
of sugar (used separately)

I teaspoon orange zest

½ cup olive oil

I cup orange juice

I ¾ cup flour

I teaspoon baking soda

¾ teaspoon salt

2 teaspoons cinnamon

Powdered sugar for dusting

DIRECTIONS

Preheat the oven to 350 degrees.

Whisk flour, baking soda, salt, and cinnamon in a bowl, and set aside.

Beat the eggs and I cup sugar on high until they are light yellow and thick. Add the orange zest, then slowly drizzle in the olive oil while mixing.

Alternate adding the dry ingredients and orange juice until well incorporated.

Pour batter into a greased 9x9-inch square or round pan, and sprinkle 2 tablespoons of sugar evenly over the top.

Bake in the oven at 350 degrees for 40-45 minutes, or until a toothpick poked in the middle of the cake comes out clean. Cool completely before slicing, then dust with powdered sugar.

SHARE WITH A FRIEND OR FAMILY,
and don't forget to say a prayer of thanksgiving
to Saint Phanourios before you enjoy!

KHOURIA CHRISTINE ROGERS

is married to Fr. John Rogers and is the mother of four. A lifelong Alaskan, she enjoys indoorsy activities like reading, baking, and not camping, although fishing is occasionally allowed (but not hiking). Christine has served twice in Kenya as an OCMC missionary and is a certified doula, as well as the author of *Spyridon's Shoes*.

Ancient Faith Publishing hopes you have enjoyed and benefited from this book. The proceeds from the sales of our books only partially cover the costs of operating our non-profit ministry—which includes both the work of **Ancient Faith Publishing** and the work of **Ancient Faith Radio.** Your financial support makes it possible to continue this ministry both in print and online. Donations are tax deductible and can be made at **www.ancientfaith.com.**

To view our other publications,
please visit our website:
store.ancientfaith.com

Bringing you Orthodox Christian music, readings, prayers, teaching, and podcasts 24 hours a day since 2004 at www.ancientfaith.com

www.ingramcontent.com/pod-product-compliance
Lightning Source LLC
Chambersburg PA
CBHW061539210726
48287CB00006B/2017